the treasure map of boys

Also by e. lockhart

The Disreputable History of Frankie Landau-Banks

Dramarama

Fly on the Wall

The Ruby Oliver novels

The Boyfriend List

The Boy Book

The Treasure Map of Boys

Real Live Boyfriends

With Lauren Myracle and Sarah Mlynowski

How to Be Bad

the treasure map of boys*

*Noel, Jackson, Finn, Hutch, Gideon –
and me, Ruby Oliver.

e.lockhart

HOT
KEY
BOOKS

This edition first published in Great Britain in 2016 by
HOT KEY BOOKS
80–81 Wimpole St, London W1G 9RE
www.hotkeybooks.com

Originally published in hardback in the US in 2009 by Delacorte Press,
an imprint of Random House Children's Books, Inc. New York

A CIP catalogue record for this book is available from the British Library.

ISBN: 978-1-4714-0600-3
also available as an ebook

1

This book is typeset in 11pt Berthold Baskerville

Printed and bound by Clays Ltd, St Ives Plc

Hot Key Books is an imprint of Bonnier Zaffre Ltd,
a Bonnier Publishing company
www.bonnierpublishing.co.uk

**For Sarah and Lauren, who made this book
so much better than it was**

contents

1.

I Am Not Always a Good Friend

Ruby,

> *In laboratories dim*
> *We bend to Fleischman's whim*
> *And suffer twice a week*
> *Horrors terrible to speak.*
> *Will you deign*
> *To ease my pain?*
> *Or will I slowly*
> *Go insane?*
> *Say you'll be my partner true*
> *In Chemistry, it's me and you.*

—written on yellow legal paper in Noel's cramped, somewhat illegible scrawl; found in my mail cubby, folded eight thousand times and with a bit of coffee spilled on one corner.

the first day back from winter break, junior year, I walked into Chem to find a head of red cabbage on every lab table. Also a juicer. Tate Prep is the kind of school where the chemistry teacher has a budget to buy fourteen juicers. I go there on scholarship.

Mr. Fleischman started the class yelling, "Happy New Year, people! Wash your hands and juice your cabbages! No fingers in the machinery!"

He was a small white man, only five foot two, with a pug nose and a large bald spot ill concealed by a comb-over. He jumped up and down more than most fifty-year-olds do and dyed what little hair he had left a shiny black. "Kitchen science!" cried Fleischman. "That's our new unit, people. Everyday chemical reactions that happen in your very own home."

I washed my hands and juiced my cabbage. Sadly, I was familiar with the procedures for juicing vegetables because my mother had started the new year by embarking on a raw food diet. Her new idea of breakfast was celery juice.

The cabbage was my cabbage and my cabbage alone because Noel was late. I'd gotten his note that morning in my mail cubby, but I hadn't seen him since before the holiday.

"Say you'll be my partner true/In Chemistry, it's me and you," he'd written.

Only now he wasn't here.

"Come to the front and get six plastic cups, protective gloves, baking soda, orange juice, liquid Drano, ammonia and vinegar," announced Fleischman. Katarina and Ariel, golden girls of the junior class, were squealing at the semi-disgusting purple glop that had formed in our juicers.

"I think I'm gonna puke from the smell," said Ariel.

"Don't puke," called Fleischman. "There's no puking allowed in chemistry. Scientists never puke."

"You smell it," said Ariel. "See how you feel."

Fleischman ignored her. "Be careful with the ammonia, people. And the Drano. I'm not seeing the gloves on your hands. The gloves go *on your hands*. Is that too much to expect you to figure out?"

I had to make three trips to the front to get everything. The third time, Ariel was there too. She held a little dish of orange juice. "Hello, Ruby," she said to me. "How was your break?"

"Good," I answered. Since the debacles of sophomore year had died down, Ariel, Katarina and Heidi all spoke to me if they *had* to. But I knew what they really thought of me.

"We skied Mount Baker over New Year's," Ariel said.

"Cool." I shrugged. Skiing is not in my budget. I spent winter break helping my dad repair cracks in his greenhouse off the side of the houseboat we live in and watching way too many movies. Dad runs an obscure and deeply earnest gardening newsletter entitled *Container Gardening for the Rare Bloom Lover.*

Why was Ariel making conversation with me, anyhow?

"Yeah," she went on. "Me, Katarina and Heidi were all about Sneaky Pete and Blueberry Cat Track."

I had no idea what she was talking about. Possibly ski trails. Possibly coffee drinks. Video games? Sexual positions?

"But Cricket skied the Chute and Kim owned Gunners Bowl," Ariel went on. "Jackson, Kyle and those guys came for New Year's. Such an excellent party."

Oh.

That was why she was telling me this.

Kim and Cricket are my ex-friends. Ariel was making sure I knew they'd all spent New Year's skiing together, which meant that Kim and Cricket were now firmly in the Katarina set.

"Spankin'," I said. Because of course it hurt that she had Kim and Cricket now. She meant it to hurt. There was nothing I could say in retaliation except something that would confuse her.[1]

"Whatever," Ariel answered, wrinkling her nose.

I went back to my table and put spoonfuls of baking soda in my cups of cabbage juice.

The cabbage juice turned blue.

"I see it's turning blue, people!" Fleischman cried, jumping. "That's good. Now add precise dropperfuls of your various other substances to the blue cabbage juice, and make a record of how many droppers it takes to return the fluid to reddish purple. Then come to conclusions about the acidic and basic contents of your ingredients."

---

[1] *Spankin'*: My new favorite word. As in, "That's a spankin' pair of lederhosen you're wearing, where did you get those?" Not as in, "Stop your whinin' or you'll get a spankin', you little brat."

I added ammonia to one of the cups. The juice turned green. Did that mean it was acidic or basic?

What were we supposed to be writing down, again?

As my lab partner, Noel was usually Captain of the Pen, while I was usually Captain of the Beaker.

Where *was* Noel? Was he really going to ask to be my lab partner and then ditch class?

And why had he *asked* to be my lab partner, anyway? We had been lab partners last term. We were obviously going to be lab partners this term too. There was no need to write a note about it.

The Drano turned my cabbage juice blue.

"Later in the term we're doing the science of baking!" Fleischman continued. "Did you people know that chemical reactions are taking place constantly in your home ovens? In your very own blenders? It's fascinating, I promise you."

The plastic gloves felt hot on my hands and I was starting to sweat in the warm lab. I was nervous about seeing Noel.

Because Noel liked me.

Or at least, he *once* liked me.

And I liked him back, if liking someone means you want to touch him whenever he's sitting next to you and he makes you laugh and you find yourself thinking about him, like, when you're alone in the shower with the door locked. If liking someone means that whenever he's in a room with you, even an auditorium or the refectory, you know exactly where he is and what he's doing, like you've got Noel radar.

Yeah.

Last fall, Noel had asked if he could kiss me. I wanted to say yes and throw myself on top of him like a kissing lunatic—but there were a thousand reasons not to. It was very complicated. So I told him no.

After that incident of extreme awkwardness, we had settled into being lab partners and occasionally eating lunch together with other people; a semi-friendship that didn't involve e-mailing, calling, writing each other notes or hanging out after school. So far, it had worked out okay. I mean, I just tried not to think about him—and most of the time I managed it.

But now, he had left me this note. And if you're like me (which hopefully you're not, because that would mean you're so neurotic you need professional help), you've read it over four times. "Say you'll be my partner true," he wrote. "In Chemistry, it's me and you."

It's verging on romantic, am I right?

"Will you deign/To ease my pain?/Or will I slowly/Go insane?"

I felt an unreasonably happy glow every time I thought of it. A glow, followed by a wave of agonizing guilt.

Glow. Guilt.

Glow. Guilt.

Glow. Guilt.

That was how my morning had been, leading up to fourth-period Chem.

Then Noel ditched class. I turned my cabbage juice a variety of shades of bluish purple, made the best notes I could and left without speaking another word to anyone.

The Thousand Reasons Not to Kiss Noel

1. Nora likes him. She told me so. True, she hasn't done anything about it except giggle when he's around and touch his shoulder too much. But she is my best friend, the only one of my old crowd who came back after the debacles of sophomore year—and she liked him first.

2. Nearly the entire population of Tate Prep thinks I am a megaslut, even though I've kissed a total of six guys in sixteen years and have never even reached the nether regions. Given my shattered reputation, I should swear off guys for a while. Like forever.

3. I am still mentally unstable thanks to said sophomore-year debacles and have to see Doctor Z to keep some semblance of sanity. I am obviously in no shape to have an actual boyfriend.

4. I have two whole friends, Meghan and Nora. If I went for Noel, and Nora hated me for it, Meghan would probably hate me too. I cannot afford to be friendless. I have been there before, thank you very much, and have no intentions of returning to complete leprosy.[2]

—entry in *The Girl Book,* my sort-of, only-sometimes-updated journal, written December of junior year.

Okay, so those are only four reasons, not a thousand. But they might as well have been a thousand, as they still resulted in me not kissing Noel and Noel not kissing me.

---

[2] *Leprosy:* It's a metaphor. Leprosy is a horrible bacterial disease that disfigures your face and rots your hands and feet. They used to send all the lepers into isolation hospitals or make them wear bells so people would hear them coming and stay clear.

I knew I shouldn't write him back when he didn't show up for Chem. Pretend you have some complete muffin for a lab partner, I told myself. If Noel were a muffin, you wouldn't write him a note just because he missed Chem.[3]

Don't write him.

You don't have to write him.

It's better not to write him.

You owe it to Nora not to write him.

Here's what I wrote:

> *Captain of the Pen,*
> *Cabbages red*
> *Became cabbage juice blue*
> *Became substances vile*
> *And of many a hue.*
>
> *I juiced and I poured;*
> *I measured stuff too.*
> *But naught came out right,*
> *For 'twas done without you.*

—Captain of the Beaker

---

3 *Muffin:* Not exactly an insult. A muffin is pleasant. It's just nothing to get cranked about. You never think, Oh, I'm going to drive out of my way so I can get that unbelievably scrumptious muffin they have at the bakery. No, you think, Unbelievably scrumptious brownie. Unbelievably scrumptious white chocolate cookie. You wouldn't go out of your way for something as ordinary as a muffin, that's what I'm explaining here.

Maybe Nora's feelings for Noel had just been a passing attraction and she hadn't really meant it.

Maybe she got over him during winter break while her family was on Grand Cayman.

Maybe Nora would fall madly in love with that guy on the basketball team who kissed her in December, or maybe she had already started seeing some hot college boyfriend she met through her brother, Gideon.

If so, it was okay to write this note.

I folded it into an origami balloon, blew it up and shoved it deep into Noel's cubby.

I Give Instructions for Ruining Your Life

How to Ruin Your Life in Nine Easy Steps:
You too can ruin your life. It isn't hard. Are you ready? Here's how.

1. Lose your first-ever boyfriend (Jackson) to your then-best friend (Kim).
2. In the process, lose your best friend. Suffer a broken heart.
3. Kiss your ex-boyfriend (Jackson).
4. Get caught kissing him. Congratulations! Now you've lost *all* your friends, because you're obviously a wench who runs around making out with other people's boyfriends.
5. Suffer panic attacks.
6. See a shrink.

7. Write a list of all the boys you ever crushed on, going back to nursery school. Because your shrink tells you to. It's for your mental health.
8. Accidentally leave a copy of said boyfriend list where people who hate you can find it.
9. Do nothing. The people who hate you find the list. Misunderstand it. And xerox it.

Voila! You are not only a leper, but also a famous slut. Life successfully ruined.

—entry in *The Girl Book,* written December of junior year.

the panic things have gotten better since I started going to see Doctor Z, my shrink. And the leprosy has abated some since Nora started being friends with me again.

But my reputation still sucks.

I showed Doctor Z what I wrote a couple of days before school started in January. She was asking me to think about *why* things happened to me. Whether any part of the debacle of my life was under my control. She read "How to Ruin Your Life" carefully, then asked: "What might you do to cause the situation to be different this year?"

"Nothing," I told her.

"Nothing?" That's not the kind of answer she likes to hear.

"I can't do anything but try to stay out of trouble."

"Then how will you stay out of trouble, Ruby?" she asked me. "There must be something you can articulate."

I thought for a moment. "I can keep away from boys," I answered.

3.

I Exist in the State of *Noboyfriend*

The state of *Noboyfriend* is not a state like New Jersey is a state. It's a state like catatonia is a state. Or depression. Or ennui.[1]

A person in the state of *Noboyfriend* is in stasis. Nothing is happening on the boy front. So little happened last month, and so little is expected to happen *next* month—or ever—that she is immobile in terms of romance. She is also afflicted with mild depression and ennui due to a lack of affection, excitement and horizontal action.

She knows, of course, that Gloria Steinem, her favorite feminist from American History and Politics last year, would tell her that "a

---

[1] *Ennui:* Another one of my new words. It means "listlessness, boredom." As in, "I would save the world, but I suffer from ennui, which forces me to lie on the couch and eat spearmint jelly candies instead."

woman without a man is like a fish without a bicycle," and she firmly believes this is true.

But maybe, depending on who she is, she wants a boyfriend anyway. Maybe the fish wants a bicycle.

The state of *Noboyfriend* is hard to leave, once you're well and firmly in. The longer you are there, the more entrenched you are. Doctors and shrinks won't be of any help. There are no pills for the state of *Noboyfriend,* no psychoanalytic diagnoses, no miracle cures.

—written by me, with help from Meghan and Nora, on a latte-stained B&O Espresso napkin, before winter break, junior year.

thankfully, I didn't have to brave the refectory alone at fifth period that first day. Meghan was already sitting at our usual lunch table. She was wearing Birkenstocks with red woolly socks, white carpenter pants and a gray hooded sweatshirt. Despite this tragic outfit, she was easily the sexiest girl in the room.

That's why she isn't popular. Girls don't actually like a person who licks her lips like a porn star in history class or distracts their boyfriends at parties by wearing a bikini in the hot tub. And Meghan has no self-awareness whatsoever, despite being the only other teenager I know who sees a shrink, so she doesn't understand how irritating some of the stuff she does is.

She doesn't bug me anymore, though. There's a lot to be said for a girl who sticks by you when hardly anyone else at school will, and the two of us secretly sing ridiculous pop songs at the top of our lungs when she carpools me to school.

"I'm over this *Noboyfriend* thing," Meghan announced as I sat down. "I decided that during Choir."

"Already?" I cracked open my peach iced tea.

"Way over it."

"Hello? You've been *Noboyfriend* for what, a month?"

"Seven weeks!" Meghan said, her mouth full of taco.

"Please don't tell me you're counting."

"Yes, I'm counting."

"Well, don't make *me* count or I may have to slit my wrists."[2]

"Roo. Suicide threats are not funny."

"Then don't make me count."

"Okay, I won't make you count . . ."

"Thanks."

". . . but only because I'm wearing white pants. The bloodstains would never come out. Ooh, there's Nora." Meghan jumped up and wrapped her arms around Nora's five-foot-eleven-inch frame. "Come sit, come sit! I need your advice!"

Nora folded herself onto the bench next to me and lifted the top piece of bread off her sandwich. "This ham doesn't smell right," she said. "Here." She shoved it toward my face. "Tell me, does that smell right?"

"No ham smells right," I told her. "It's a hunk of dead pig."

"Veggie." She laughed. "Here, Meghan, smell it."

---

[2] I had been *Noboyfriend* for thirty-nine weeks at that point.

Meghan smelled and shook her head. "Don't eat it. I need both of you alive to help me leave the state of *Noboyfriend*."

"What about me?" Nora asked. "I want to leave it too."[3]

"Of course. This should be the end of *Noboyfriend* for all of us. Especially because it's never too early to think about Spring Fling."

I moaned. "It is *too* too early."

"Fine. Only I think it would be great to have a boyfriend for Spring Fling. Not just a date, but like a real boyfriend to be in love with."

This is a perfect example of how Meghan's brain works. She can think that she'd like to work toward being *in love* by the time a particular dance comes around, even though she doesn't have so much as a crush on any particular boy at school. And she wants to be in love not really to be in love, but to maximize romance on the mini-yacht dance Tate Prep throws every April. I mean, what kind of person has that for a goal, anyhow, instead of, I don't know, making varsity lacrosse or a 2100 on the SAT?

"And who is this real boyfriend going to be?" I asked Meghan.

---

[3] Nora is in a state of perpetual *Noboyfriend*—only pretty much without catatonia, depression or ennui. It has been sixteen and a half *years* of *Noboyfriend* for Nora, though she does appear to like boys rather than, you know, girls. She is possessed of a good heart, beautiful dark curls, the ability to bake *and* talk basketball simultaneously, plus enormous hooters and stable mental health—really, everything a guy could want.

But still: *Noboyfriend*.

"I don't know. That's what I need help with. Who would be good for me?"

"Meghan!"

"What?"

"Who do you *like*?"

She shrugged. "I'm ruling out seniors," she said. "The last thing I need is another guy who's going off to college. But I'm having trouble when I look at the juniors, too." She reached into her backpack and pulled out the school directory, which contained everyone's name, address and school photo from the previous year. She flipped it open to the junior class page and handed it to me. "I've known these guys since kindergarten. We all have. It might be biologically impossible for me to go out with any of them. Unless you see something I haven't."

Nora looked over my shoulder. "Look at Noel's hair," she said, pointing to his photo.

I laughed. He was wearing a ridiculous amount of hair gel.

I scanned the photos. Tate Prep is a small school with a serious dearth of decent guys: it was all Neanderthals, sporty muffins and Future Doctors of America, or guys in the gaming club and guys who hadn't hit puberty yet, ineligible for reasons I think must be obvious. That was pretty much it.

"How about Hutch?" I said.

John Hutchinson (aka Hutch) has been at Tate since kindergarten. He's a leper due to tragic skin and a marked tendency to quote retro heavy-metal lyrics in place of making sane conversation, but now that I got to know him this past fall, I don't think he's so bad. He became my dad's gardening assistant last year. They work together in the greenhouse on the southern side of our houseboat, and even though Hutch is even more lacking in human relationship skills than I am, he's a nice guy. Noel likes him too.

Meghan wrinkled her nose. "I like a guy more athletic than Hutch," she said diplomatically. Because Hutch is not an attractive physical specimen.

"This is bad news," said Nora, shaking her head over the directory. "You may have to look at sophomores."

"We *are* allowed to go out with guys outside of Tate, you know," I said. "There's no law against it."

Meghan sniffed. "When would I even meet such a guy? I have tennis team starting soon; I have therapy. College visits on weekends. The most important thing in life, and I don't even have time for it, really."

"Boyfriends are not the most important thing in life," said Nora. "They can't be."

"Not boyfriends. Love."

I shook my head. "You are a warped little bunny, my friend."

"Seriously," Meghan persisted. "What's more important than love? Because it's not tennis team, I'm telling you that right now."

"So you have to look at the sophomores," Nora said.

I groaned.

"Why not?" Nora went on. "Boys do it all the time. I don't want to think about how many junior and senior guys are going out with sophomore girls right now. It might as well be the other way around."

Meghan shot a glance over to a sophomore table, where two six-foot boys were leaning back in their chairs. One threw a raisin at the other, who fell out of his chair. Knocked spineless by a raisin.

"They're taller than they used to be," she said thoughtfully.

"Operation Sophomore Love," I said. "That's your project, right there."

●

Normally after school I have sports practice or therapy or I go to my internship at the Woodland Park Zoo, where I work in the penguin exhibit and the Family Farm area. But I was sitting out lacrosse this term since there was no way I'd make varsity goalie, and the internship hadn't started again yet.

These circumstances meant I was free after school to go shopping with my mother. I needed a coat and a couple of sweaters. The weather was colder than usual that winter, and I'd gained a few inches since sophomore year. She picked me up in the Honda.

My mother is more bohemian than the other mothers at Tate Prep. Other mothers tend to be brain surgeons, lawyers or homemakers, while Elaine Oliver is a semisuccessful performance artist and part-time copy editor who could easily earn a merit badge for annoying babble. Despite her artsy lifestyle and minimal income, she would still like to dress me as the kind of child she wishes she had.

That is, wholesome and well-adjusted.

Mom took me to the BP department of Nordstrom because Grandma Suzette gave her a gift certificate there for Christmas. Also, I suspect, because Nordstrom is safely in the mall, where there are no vintage shops for me to wander into.

We strolled through the aisles of fresh, brightly colored sweaters and stacks of jeans. Mom waved an aqua turtleneck at me. It was decorated with an appliqué of a poodle. "This is your style, isn't it, Roo?"

"It's aqua. Have you ever seen me wear aqua?"

"It would bring out your eyes."

"And have you ever seen me wear a turtleneck?"

"No," she admitted. "But my neck is always cold in the middle of winter. Isn't yours?"

"No."

"I thought you'd like it because it's vintage-y. See, with the poodle? People used to wear skirts with poodles on them in the fifties."

I took hold of the foul turtleneck. Next, she showed me a white wool coat decorated with brown anchors and curlicues of nautical rope.

"This is very you," she said, smiling proudly at her find. "Isn't it?"

Anchors?

"It has a sense of irony," she continued. "I know you like irony. Plus it'll be warm around your neck. Try it on."

It didn't have a sense of irony. Those were completely unironic anchors.

While Mom was grabbing fuzzy pullovers in colors

that radiated solid mental health, I picked up a navy blue hoodie and a plain black cardigan, in case she was going to insist we complete our shopping here.

She shoved herself into the dressing room with me, her mane of frizzy dark hair so close that when I took off my shirt I actually brushed against it with my bare body. She clucked her tongue upon seeing me in the poodle turtleneck. "You look beautiful!" she told me. "Oh, it clings to all the right places."

Ag.

"I don't know why you're always covering your body with bowling shirts that used to belong to some old plumber," my mother went on. "It's self-sabotage, don't you think?"

"No."

"You should talk to Doctor Z about it."

"About how I like vintage clothes?"

"Old things, things other people have discarded. Stuff that's shapeless and falling apart."

"And that shows what?" I prodded.

"That *you* feel discarded! That you don't feel light and sunny. You never wear pink or yellow, Ruby."

"Mom."

"What?"

"Look in the mirror."

She looked. "I'm wearing all black, so what? That's not the point. I'm forty-five years old."

"You're forty-seven."

She harrumphed. "Whatever age I am, it's an age where black looks good on me. And besides, all black is very stylish. You, you buy these old dresses that have practically no shape and the buttons falling off them, when you could spend the same money on this poodle sweater that shows off your breasts so nicely."

Did she have to say *breasts*?

"You get your breasts from my side the family," my mother said. "I have nice breasts."

She owned a book called *Empower Your Girl Child,* which I had secretly read. It told her that as the parent of a teenager she should role-model bodily self-confidence. "Grandma Suzette has no breasts to speak of," Mom continued. "She's flat as a table. Not that there's anything wrong with that. It can be very attractive. Now try this coral angora one with the cute bow. Look, it says 'fresh' on the collar in rhinestones. Isn't that similar to those beaded sweaters you like?"

I pulled off the turtleneck and my mom reached out a clammy hand and grabbed my naked arm.

"What?"

She stood to examine my shoulder. "Do you know you have some pimples on your back?" She ran her hand over the area.

Did she have to say *pimples?* Couldn't she just say I was breaking out or having some skin trouble?

Pimples. Breasts. Pimples. Breasts. It was like the woman was walking around with a vocab list and consulting it regularly: *Uncomfortable Words Relating to the Physical Changes of Adolescence.*

"You don't need to fondle them," I told her.

She removed her hand and sat back down. "It's normal to have pimples when you're sixteen."

"Thanks for the tidbit. And you wonder why I have to go the shrink."

She barked with laughter. "It's not because of *me,* you can be sure of that."

"Right." I pulled the coral angora rhinestone thing over my head so as not to be standing there in my bra anymore, giving her an eyeful of my bad skin.

"Really. It's your father. He's inconsistent with you. I'm sure you've noticed that. And I love him, but he does have quite a few inhibitions of his own. There's no denying it. Ooh, look at yourself in the mirror!"

I resembled a tulip with bling.

"Try it with the anchor coat," she commanded.

Fine. I put on the anchor coat.

"Roo, you have no idea how beautiful you are," Mom gushed. "Now, did you see they have this same angora in lime? It says 'Charmant' on the collar, though."

Ag, ag and more ag.

"Run out and it get it, why don't you?" she said. "I want to see how it looks with your eyes."

"Why don't you go?" I whined.

She had her cell phone out. "I'm calling Dad, that's why. I have to tell him to check the raw peanuts that are soaking in the fridge. Did you know my recipe actually says to take them out when they're the size of border collie testicles? I swear to you, I'm not making that up. It's straight out of the peanut goulash recipe."

If she wanted me to go away, discussion of peanut goulash and border collie testicles was a good way to make it happen. I went to look for the "charmant" angora, tags from the unironic anchor coat flapping behind me.

I had just found the table where the lime green excrescence was folded neatly in a stack and was searching for my size when a voice murmured my name, near my ear.

"Hey there, Roo."

My ex-boyfriend. Jackson Clarke.

Here in the BP section of Nordstrom. Wearing the jacket I bought him for Christmas a year ago.

We generally avoided each other as much as possible.

"That's Ms. Roo to you," I said.

Why, oh, why did I have to be blinged-up-angora-tulip-unironic-anchor person just when Jackson was wandering the BP? Because even if a girl is completely over her ex-boyfriend, *and* even if he has a girlfriend he's been with for ten months, *and* even if he's not even the person she thought he was, back when they were together—even if all those things are true, she still wants to be gorgeous and desirable every time she sees him.

She still wants him to look at her and think, Oh, man, I messed that up. She is unbelievably hot.

Jackson looked me up and down. "Shopping?"

"For superhero disguises," I said, to explain my outfit.

He raised his eyebrows.

"You know," I went on, "how superheroes need to have nerdy alter egos that help them go through life with no one suspecting their secret awesomeness?"

He nodded. "Like Meimi in Saint Tail." Jackson had a thing for anime.[4]

"Like Superman," I said. "So what do you think? Will this outfit delude the average men and women of America into thinking I couldn't possibly wield superpowers?"

He laughed. "You do look funny," he said.

Ouch.

Jackson leaned in to read my rhinestone collar. "Or should I say, you look *fresh*?"

"Why are you here, anyway?" I asked him.

But before he could answer, I realized what the answer had to be.

He was here with Kim. She was probably changing in the dressing room next to mine, listening to my mother talk about my breasts and my pimples and my psychological problems and also border collie testicles.

"Oh, I'm looking for a coat with anchors," he told me. "Do you know where I could find something like that? Something nautical, with maybe some curly rope on it?"

"Shut up."

"Don't be fresh with me."

"That's not even funny."

"Is too." He turned his grin on me.

I shook my head. "You've lost your touch. Is Kim in the changing room?"

---

4 *Anime:* Japanese animation. Jackson is obsessed with it, but me—not so much. Boring, boring, boring. Still, I've seen a lot of anime movies, because when Jackson and I were together, he always, always got to pick the film.

"I'm here with Dempsey. She has a gift certificate. I'm playing chauffeur."

I exhaled. Dempsey is his sister. She's an eighth grader. The Tate middle school has a different campus from the upper school, so I hadn't seen her since Jackson and I were going out—but suddenly, there she was next to me, looking at the lime angora "charmant" sweater in my hand and saying, "Hi, Ruby, wow, do you like that sweater? It's way sweet. Ooh, you have the coral one on already, that looks so cute on you, are you gonna buy it? Because if you're not, do you mind if I try it on? I have a gift certificate, did doofus-head tell you that?"

"Hi, Dempsey," I said.

"I haven't seen you like, wow, since I was a seventh grader," Dempsey babbled. "I love your hair. Do you think I should get bangs? I don't think I can work bangs. It takes a face like yours to work the bangs." She grabbed the front of her hair and pulled it up so that the ends hung down over her eyebrows. "What do you think?"

"You could work the bangs," I said. "And I'm not getting either of these angoras. They're all yours."

But she had already lost interest in the angoras and was touching an argyle sweater vest. "Is argyle out yet?" she asked me.

I shrugged.

"And what do you think about Jackson being single again?" Dempsey asked.

I looked at Jackson. He was staring at his feet with his hands shoved in the front pocket of his sweatshirt.

He wasn't single before winter break. He was with Kim. He'd been with Kim since last spring.

"News to me," I said, my heart thudding.

"He and Kim broke up at lunch today," Dempsey explained. "I thought you'd know."

Why would she think I'd know? Did Dempsey think people like Cricket and Kim still talked to me?

"*Goodbye,* Dempsey." This from Jackson, with a threat in his voice.

"I was hoping you might tell me details," she went on, ignoring him. "He wouldn't explain what happened. I know it has to be his fault, though. No offense, but I don't know why anyone would go out with him in the first place." Dempsey fingered a rayon shirt. "He's not even cute and his room is disgusting."

That was untrue. Jackson was desperately cute. Dark brown hair curling at his neck. Soft freckles. Tall. Raspy voice. Narrow hips.

"She really likes you," I said to Jackson, deadpan. "You must be a great big brother."

"Don't listen to anything she says," he told me.

"I'm telling the truth!" cried Dempsey. "You told me yourself it was over with Kim!"

"My mom is waiting for me," I said, grabbing a stack of heinous sweaters off the table. "I gotta go."

●

I could hear my mother long before I reached the changing room, where she was still sitting. Elaine Oliver is one of those people who thinks she needs to yell into a cell phone and cannot imagine that anyone else might hear her conversation. "I'm stiff from that yoga class Juana made me go to!" she was shouting, presumably to Dad. "I did something to my groin area. . . . Sure, you can massage it later."

I opened the door to the dressing room.

"I gotta go, Kevin, Roo is back. Oh, will you get her some benzoyl peroxide at the drugstore when you pick up the paper towels? She's got some pimples that look like they could use some treatment. . . . Love you too. Bye."

I tried on ugly sweater after ugly sweater, not listening to my mother's commentary, not looking at myself in the mirror, thinking: Jackson and Kim broke up.

Just today at lunch.

While I was eating salad with fried Chinese noodles.

While I was talking to Meghan about whether I should

play lacrosse this spring.

Ten months ago, he had left me for her.

Ten months ago, she had left me for him.

Eight gazillion therapy sessions later, I finally didn't care. They were together. That was how the world was.

I could handle the world that way.

And now, it wasn't that way anymore. Everything had changed while I was drinking peach iced tea in the refectory.

●

Though I managed to avoid the poodle turtleneck in favor of the navy hoodie, I was too weakened by the situation to stop my mother from buying me the coat with anchors.

the reason a popular senior girl like Gwen Archer was writing me a note in first period French V was this: due to circumstances semi–beyond my control, I was the member of the junior class with the most bake-sale experience. Every year before the winter holidays, the Tate Prep upperclassmen organize this Charity Holiday Bake Sale (CHuBS) to benefit a homeless shelter in downtown Seattle; every year all students are also required to log a certain number of community service hours. I joined CHuBS when I was a sophomore, shockingly behind on service and deluded by romantic fantasies of baking for Jackson. I had this idea that I would secure his undying love by means of chocolate-cream-cheese goodness.

Not so much.

Anyway, I did well in CHuBS even though I'm completely unskilled in the kitchen. I had good ideas for cupcakes, which was important because despite its charitable mission, the sale is really a competition: whose adorable creation can best attract the gluttons of the Tate Prep Universe? Girls bring in reindeer cookies with pretzels for horns. Seven-layer ultimate fudge. Santa Claus cupcakes. Sugar cookies baked onto Popsicle sticks.

December of junior year, Gwen Archer–now head of CHuBS and one of those hearty Future Doctors of America so prevalent at Tate Prep–corralled me into a second season of bake-sale insanity. Volunteers were scarce, and Gwen asked me to recruit. She must have been so blinkered into her world of Senior Committee, tennis team and community service perkiness that she didn't bother to read the things written on the walls of the girls' bathrooms or notice the blue-green spots of leprosy[1] that covered my body.

Meghan hadn't done a single service hour all year, and we're required to do forty, so she was on board. Nora, although she is completely the person who volunteers for all kinds of do-good projects through her church without even trying to snag school credit for them, agreed to help too. She *likes* to bake. So the three of us had worked the December bake sale together junior year.

Archer's idea of CHuBS was all about marshmallow sculptures. She forced us to make them. Did you know that with a pair of kitchen scissors, some white frosting, an assortment of adorably small candies and many, many hours of labor, ordinary marshmallows can be transformed into miniature snowmen who sit atop cupcakes, wearing jolly gummy hats, M&M buttons and maniacal licorice smiles?

They can.

I myself have made them in Archer's enormous yellow kitchen. I have also bought one, eaten half of it and thrown the rest in the garbage. Because marshmallows, unless heavily toasted in s'mores, are not as good as I thought they were in first grade.

In fact, they're gross.

---

[1] More on *leprosy:* I finally Googled it. Turns out that despite its reputation, leprosy is not really that contagious, as far as diseases go. And the blue-green spots I keep talking about? They're not actually blue-green. In other words, *leper* is actually a sucky metaphor for a social pariah like myself. I will have to think of a new word.

Go on, see for yourself. Eat a raw marshmallow and tell me you actually want to eat another one.

There were a lot of snowmen in the garbage can near the bake sale table at the end of the first day, actually, but Archer was not discouraged. They had sold well, after all, and since the sale lasted a week, her next project involved handmade marshmallows shaped like stars. Then marshmallow Santas and cupcakes shaped like turkeys.

The whole December CHuBS experience had been like shopping with my mother. I put in all this time and energy and ended up with something other people thought was adorable but made *me* want to chunder. So when I got Archer's note in January of junior year, at first I thought: No way.

1. I'm actually not a good baker.

2. I've done all my service already.

3. If I run Baby CHuBS now, I'll be expected to run Big CHuBS when I'm a senior. No way can a roly-poly[2] like me manage to recruit a whole gaggle of underclassmen to do the grunt work of the weeklong December sale.

4. I am not a person who wants anything to do with marshmallow sculpture projects.

5. And–

---

[2] *Roly-poly.* The derogatory term formerly known as *leper.* Technically, a bug called a woodlouse. You have the same response to a roly-poly as to a leper: "Ugh, there's a roly-poly here [on my plate, on my arm, on this bench, whatever]—let's move away." Only, it's nicer, because roly-polies are actually a tiny bit cute, plus they have a good name, so while the Tate Universe may not rate

I interrupted my own thoughts. Because this was a chance, actually. A chance to reject the dominant Tate Prep aesthetic of marshmallow sculpture in favor of my own roly-poly agenda.

What exactly that agenda was, I didn't know.

Something different.

Something uncute.

Something delicious, maybe.

I told Archer yes.

---

them, a few discerning roly-poly lovers will see their true merits and refuse to shun them.

P.S. There is also a kind of dessert called a roly-poly made with jam. That is not what I am talking about.

5.

I Fixate on a Poncho

tuesday, Noel turned up in my Art History elective. Ms. Harada was showing slides, and he slid into the seat next to me shortly after the lecture started.

He was wearing steel-toed combat boots and a Daffy Duck T-shirt over a black thermal.[1] His blond hair was free of gel (unusual for him) and flopped across his forehead.

I reminded myself to look at the art.

His profile, lit by the glow from the projector, seemed so pure, so clean. Like the delicate lines of his face had been cut from marble.

---

[1] Also pants, of course, lest your imagination get away with you. He was wearing pants.

I've missed him, I thought. Even though we hadn't spent much time together before the break.

Even though I hadn't known I was missing him.

Noel flipped open his yellow legal pad and scrawled something across the top: "My hair looks weird, I know."

He had noticed me staring at him. And yes, actually, his hair did look weird, but the rest of him was . . . well, he was Noel. I was cranked to see him; what did hair matter?

I turned to a new page in my notebook and wrote: Do you bake?

Noel: Why do you want to know?

Me: Well, do you?

Noel: I reserve the right to remain silent until you answer my question.

Me: I am accidentally in charge of a bake sale.

Noel: Bake sale like the thing in December with marshmallow snowmen?

Me: We had snow women, too. With pink frosting bikini tops.

Noel: Excuse me while I retch.

Me: We also had snow dogs.

Noel: If by "bake" you mean do I construct marshmallow snow dogs, then no. I do not. My talents lie elsewhere.

Me: Not so fast! My policy is anti-marshmallow.

Noel: You seriously want me to make something for your sale?

I had written the first thing that popped into my head that wasn't about Noel's hair, since that didn't seem to be a good direction for the conversation to go.

But yes. I wanted him to.

Me: Do you know how to bake? Lots of boys don't.
Noel: I am not lots of boys.
Me: Actually, I don't know how to bake, either. Nora helps me.
Noel: What do you mean, "either"? I didn't say I couldn't bake.
Me: Can you?
Noel: Talk later. I want to hear what Harada is saying about Greek sculpture. This could be educational!
Me: Ha ha.

He grinned and flipped his legal pad shut, then remembered he was supposed to be taking notes and flipped it open again to a fresh page.

He spent the rest of the class period writing down facts about Greek sculpture. Afterward, he said he had a meeting with his college counselor and disappeared.

I felt bereft.

How could he write me that Chem class note and then brush me off?

What was up?

•

"It was not a pretty situation in Twentieth-Century Am Lit today," I told Doctor Z after school.[2] We sat in her office, which is housed in a large, unfriendly compound full of dermatologists and orthodontists and probably even philatelists[3] and atheists on the upper floors. I hate the

---

[2] Just in case you're confused, we don't have the same classes every day at Tate.
[3] *Philatelists:* Big word for stamp collectors. I only know it because my dad's crazy friend Greg is an amateur philatelist. He has a panic disorder and never

building, with its medical, astringent smell, but once you're inside her door, she's made it cozy. There's a red couch for me and a brown upholstered chair for Doctor Z. Some masks and landscape paintings on the walls. A box of tissues on the coffee table.

Doctor Z was wearing a new poncho. It must have been a Christmas gift—or Hanukkah, or whatever holiday she celebrated. I saw the woman every week and had no idea what religion she was. I didn't know if she was married, either, though I wondered about it all the time.

What was her real life like? What did she do in her spare time? Her last name is Zaczkowski, which I think is Polish, and her skin is medium-brown African American. She's gently plump and has a penchant for handmade crafty-type sweaters and hippie sandals.

This poncho was a step out, even for her. It was made of velvety bright orange yarn and had sparkle fringe at the bottom.

It was very distracting.

How was I supposed to concentrate on my mental health when my therapist was encased in orange sparkle madness?

I felt a nearly uncontrollable urge to ask her if there was a reason for her poncho, though I knew doing so would cause nothing but problems. Plus, I've been in

---

leaves the house. That's what will happen to me if my panic attacks get too bad. I'll get scared to leave the house and I'll stop functioning and people who want to visit me will have to come over and bring me Chinese food. I'll probably even start thinking stamps are actually interesting—which is the kind of thing that happens to you when you never, *ever* go anywhere.

therapy long enough to be able to figure out on my own that I had this desire to talk about her poncho because:

1. I wanted to make myself feel superior to someone, anyone, after a crap day at school. Or

2. I was uncomfortable in therapy again after two weeks of winter break and felt the need to get the upper hand in the situation. Or

3. I was angry at Doctor Z just for existing and asking me personal questions, and being obnoxious about her poncho would be a form of retaliation. Or

4. I'd like to know more about Doctor Z and who the heck she is in real life, only I'm not supposed to ask, and the poncho had become a symbol of that forbidden curiosity. Or

5. Something was bothering me that I was scared to talk about, so my mind was repressing it massively and just thinking: Poncho! Poncho! Poncho! all the time. Or

6. All of the above.

"You seem distracted, Ruby," Doctor Z said, popping a piece of Nicorette gum.[4]

"What?"

"You started talking about your American Lit class, but then you drifted off."

Poncho! Poncho! Poncho!

"Oh, it's not important," I told her. "I'm doing some

---

[4] That is the one thing I know for certain about her life outside therapy. Doctor Z must smoke like a fiend, because she's never without the Nicorette.

Reginald today.[5] Even though I should be over the whole thing already."

"There's no 'should' about something like that," Doctor Z said patiently. "Whatever you feel is valid. We all grieve on our own schedules."

"Reginald."

She smiled. "We all *Reginald* on our own schedules. Do you have a sense of what might have triggered your Reginald?"

Poncho! Poncho! Poncho!

"Ruby?"

Poncho! "Oh. Um. Yeah. Going back to school is hard. Because I managed to kind of forget the existence of certain people over break, and now they're in my Am Lit class."

"What certain people?" Doctor Z leaned forward.

39

"I was expecting it to be my favorite class," I went on. "Because it's taught by Mr. Wallace and I'm going to like Edith Wharton.[6] But when I walked into the room, there they were."

"Who?"

---

5 *Reginald:* Not a normal therapeutic term, just in case you're wondering. *Reginald* is what Doctor Z and I have agreed to call the grieving process, meaning me grieving over losing all my friends and the other debacles of last year. Only, the phrase *grieving process* gives me hives. So we call it Reginald.

6 Edith Wharton. Mr. Wallace had told me *The House of Mirth* would be on the syllabus second term, and I knew from watching the movie that it's about the social downfall of a popular woman whose friends and boyfriends all desert her and she ends up a roly-poly pauper and eventually dead.

So basically, story of my life.

Except the dead part, hopefully.

"Cricket McCall, Ariel Olivieri, Katarina Dolgen. Kim Yamamoto. And Nora. Sitting together."

Doctor Z nodded understandingly. "Did you want to join them?"

"No."

Silence.

"I didn't," I protested. "Why would I want to sit with people who don't like me? I mean, some of them tolerate me, but that's about it, and I may be insane but I'm way over wanting to hang out with people who would write stuff about me on bathroom walls."[7]

"I thought you said Nora was with them."

"She was."

"How did that make you feel?"

"Nora is peaceful," I explained. "Nora is a good person. She never takes sides. So Nora is still friends with Kim and Cricket."

"Uh-huh."

"I mean, she didn't know I had Am Lit third period

---

[7] Yeah. They did. It's still there, in stall number three of the main building girls' bathroom:

Ruby Oliver is a _____ . (fill in the blank)
   Lousy friend.
   Fantasist.
   Slut . . .
   Trollop.
   Hussy.
   Tart.
   Chippie.
I know Kim's and Cricket's writing as well as I know my own.

Tuesdays, so she was perfectly entitled to sit by them. She had no way of knowing I'd be left out."

"I'm hearing that you don't want to blame her."

Ag. I hate it when Doctor Z does that shrinky thing of repeating back to me what she hears. Poncho! Poncho! Poncho!

"Anyway," I said. "We're not fifteen anymore. No one was going to openly shun me. They all mumbled 'hello' or whatever and I slunk over to the geeky spot right next to Mr. Wallace."

"Did you have any feelings about that?"

"No."

"Anything you hoped or wished would happen?"

"No."

We sat in silence.

"What else?" Doctor Z finally asked.

"I talked to Wallace," I said. "About how Chelsea Lefferts was still going to be varsity goalie so I'm sitting out lacrosse this year. About my internship at the zoo and how I'm cranked to see the llamas and the goats on Friday. He asked questions about what I do in the Family Farm area. Small talk, really. I was actually trying to hear what Kim was saying across the table."[8]

---

[8] What I didn't tell Doctor Z: I am obviously certifiable, because all through this conversation with Mr. Wallace about lacrosse and the zoo internship, *and* while I was trying to listen to what Kim saying at the other end of the table, I was also secretly trying to look down the open collar of my teacher's shirt to see chest hair.

Because I am hormonally deranged, that's why.

Wallace is nearly thirty. Plus, he's married.

Plus, he's my teacher. Gross.

Except, I still looked.

How come?"

"It sounded like she was explaining about her breakup with Jackson."

"Ahh." A small smile played around Doctor Z's mouth. "So *that's* what this is about."

"What?" Poncho! Poncho! Poncho!

"You were diverting my attention."

"From what?"

"We spent a bunch of our session today talking about Nora. But really, we were talking about Jackson. Weren't we?"

She looked so pleased.

I hate it when she's right.

Nora called me that evening around seven. She didn't have lunch the same time as me on Tuesdays, so I had barely seen her since Am Lit.

"Please don't be mad at me for sitting with those guys in class," she said as soon as I answered.

I wasn't mad exactly. I just—I had wanted her to sit with me.

Only, how can you ask without sounding like a pathetic roly-poly? Please will you sit with me, Nora, instead of them? Pretty please?

Ag.

"I'll sit with you from now on," Nora told me. Without me asking.

And that's why I love Nora. She understands the fragility of other human beings and wants to make them feel better. She really does.

"Come over and we can get in the hot tub," she said. "I'll call Meghan."

It was too early in the term to have any homework besides Pre-Cal, so Meghan picked me up in her Jeep. Half an hour later we were in the Van Deusens' hot tub on the back deck of their huge but still-cluttered house, drinking pop and looking at each other through the steam that rose from the wooden tub into the cold night air.

I looked at Meghan, sitting on the edge in her bikini with her hair knotted on top of her head, and Nora in a tank top and boxer shorts, submerged in the hot water with only her head and her big feet sticking out, and I thought, I have a good life.

If only I can manage not to ruin it.

Which meant, I have a good life. If only I can manage to forget about boys.

Noel. Jackson. Pretty much all boys.

If I remain in the state of *Noboyfriend* forever, everything will be okay. Nora will still love me.

"Did you see that note from Archer I put in your mail cubby?" I asked.

Nora groaned. "Baby CHuBS? That's the stupidest name I ever heard."

"I know," I told her. "But Meghan's doing it with me."

"Didn't we just do a bake sale in December?" asked Nora, wiggling her toes.

"Yes, but we need you," coaxed Meghan. "You're the only one who knows how to bake. Plus, we can call ourselves cochairs now. It will look good for college applications."

"It's hardly baking," snorted Nora. "It's snipping marshmallows and bits of Fruit Roll-Up into shapes."

"But don't you think we could do something better now that I'm in charge?" I said. "I mean, don't you think the student body of Tate Prep could be collectively convinced to eschew cute but disgusting marshmallow confections in favor of true deliciousness?"

"Speak English, Roo," said Meghan.

I splashed her.

"Fine," said Nora. "You talked me into it with your ridiculous vocabulary."

"Spankin'," I said. "See, Meghan? Nora appreciates me."

"You promise no marshmallows?" Nora asked.

"I promise. Deliciousness only."

"All right, then."

Meghan changed the subject. "Nora, tell us all about the whole Kim-Jackson breakup thing," she said, leaning forward.

I held my breath, waiting to hear what Nora would say.

"Kim's shattered." Nora took a sip of her ginger ale.

"Really? What did Jackson do?" I asked, trying to sound like it didn't matter to me, he'd never been *my* boyfriend.

Nora heaved herself onto the edge of the hot tub. "I can't get into the details," she said, and sighed. "I promised her I wouldn't. She doesn't want everyone knowing all about it."

"Oh."

My intense curiosity must have showed on my face,

because Nora added: "It's not that I don't trust you guys, it's just—it's not my secret. It's Kim's."

I ached to know. After seeing them holding hands in the hallway. After watching him stroke her hair the way he used to stroke mine. After feeling like a blade was going through my chest every time I saw them together, for so many months—I almost felt I *deserved* to know what had happened.

"All you really need to know is, she's better off without him," Nora continued. "He made her feel insecure all the time. Like something else was always more important than she was."

I remembered that feeling. I used to dread being invited to parties because if I went, I'd be miserable while Jackson chatted in a dark corner with some girl from another school—but if I didn't go, it seemed like maybe he'd end up doing something more in that dark corner, and then I'd hate myself for even thinking such a thing and feel like I must be insane possessive untrusting jealous girl. It was a cycle.

But I always figured Kim was different. Jackson left me for her because she was the one he loved.

"She was so sure he was 'the one,' " I couldn't help saying.

"Well, he's turned out not to be," said Nora. "He broke up with her *at school*. Can you believe it? And then he told her, 'No hard feelings.' "

"What did she say to *that*?" Meghan asked.

"She said, 'You're breaking up with me. I'm allowed to have hard feelings, you fuckhead.' "

Meghan laughed.

Nora plunged back into the tub. When her head came back up, she said, "That's it, we have to change the subject now."

Meghan started talking about her ex-boyfriend Bick, who was now at Harvard smoking pot and being pretentious, and I appreciated Nora's loyalty, so I didn't ask anything else about Jackson and Kim. But I couldn't concentrate on the conversation.

One part of me felt sympathy. Poor Kim. Even though Jackson had chosen her over me, still she was someone I used to love, and I felt sorry for her, knowing she was shattered.

One part of me felt shock. Because the idea that Jackson had made Kim feel insecure just like he'd made *me* feel insecure—I couldn't quite believe it. He had given her a cashmere sweater. He had begged her forgiveness when she came back from Tokyo. He had written her romantic letters. I knew these things were true, and yet . . . she had felt just like I had. Like she hadn't really mattered to him.

Then one tiny, shameful part of me thought:

He doesn't love her.

He never loved her.

Yay.

"I can't believe she called him a fuckhead," I finally said.

6.

I Am a Reluctant Bodyguard

Roo,

Here's a true confession.

I skipped Chemistry first day back for a reason.

A reason involving Ariel Olivieri.

On the rebound from her breakup with Shiv.

A reason involving a chance encounter at Bailey/Coy Books the last day of winter break.

Her giving me a ride home in the rain.

And physical contact that now I shudder to recall.

My advance spies tell me AO may be up for a repeat.

No repeat is going to be happening.

I am filled with remorse and a general sense of yuckiness

at the memory of what I did under the influence of an atmospheric rainstorm, random hormones and a general sense of being alone on the planet.

I could not face Chem first day back. But I also can't ditch class for the rest of the term without incurring the wrath of Fleischman, so I have a proposition for you. I need your protection from the undesired advances of AO.

I wish to employ your services as bodyguard, and will pay you gladly in Fruit Roll-Ups.

I leave this note unsigned, as it is highly incriminating. I suggest you eat it when the contents have been memorized.

—written in Noel's scribble on yellow legal paper, folded in quarters, with the word "Top-secret" across the outside.

In all the years we've been at school together, Ariel Olivieri's mail cubby has always been directly next to mine—Ruby Oliver. More than one painful situation has occurred due to this proximity. Someone with my history knows better than to leave such an explosive note in a public mail cubby—not even taking into account it's being a public mail cubby *directly next to* the mail cubby of the person being discussed in the note—but Noel was untraumatized by the dramas of the Tate Universe and therefore fairly stupid in this regard.

I ripped the note into tiny shreds and flushed the pieces down the toilet, thinking how Noel was the third guy who had liked me and then liked Ariel instead. Sure, one was in

4.

I Become a Baby CHuB

Oliver,

Welcome back from break.

The Senior Committee wants to have an extra CHuBS this year!!! Since the winter one was so successful. During the week-long sale, we raised more than $2,000 for the shelter. If we have a new one on Parents' Day, we can do some good business. But here's the deal: none of the seniors has time, what with prom and graduation planning, so we want the juniors to run it.

We thought of such a cute name for you guys: Baby CHuBS. It could have an Easter theme.

What do you think??? Come find me after class and we can chat.

—Gwen Archer

—written on white notebook paper with ballpoint, in round hand-writing; folded in thirds like a business letter and passed to me under the table during French V.

fourth grade and one was freshman year. But still. Three guys.[1]

Were Ariel and I similar? Aside from being average height with a muscular build and brown hair—no. Ariel was pretty in a warm, dimpled, blue-jean way, whereas on a good day I was pretty in a sharp, eyeglasses, fishnet-stocking way. As for social status, she was golden and I was a roly-poly; and as for personality, she was a vacant shell decorated with charming mannerisms and occasional mild bitchiness, while I was—I don't know what I was.

Neurotic.

Maybe I ought to highlight my hair, I thought. Maybe I should wear jeans that cling to my butt. Maybe if I didn't come to school in torn fishnets and clunky Mary Janes people wouldn't always be choosing Ariel over me.[2]

Ag. No.

Thoughts like this are exactly why I'm too neurotic to have a boyfriend.

Anyway, Noel had kissed Ariel. At the very least. There had been "physical contact." And even though he said he shuddered to recall it and there would be no

---

[1] For the record, the two boys were Hutch (fourth grade) and Shiv (freshman year).

Yes, Hutch. Certified retro-metal roly-poly and my dad's gardening assistant.

No, I don't want to talk about it.

[2] Movies in which a makeover facilitates love: *Grease; Pretty Woman; Sabrina* (both versions); *Working Girl; Clueless; The Breakfast Club; My Fair Lady; She's All That; The Mirror Has Two Faces; Cinderella; Now, Voyager; Strictly Ballroom; Miss Congeniality; Moonstruck; The Princess Diaries; Never Been Kissed.*

repeats, I still couldn't help thinking of his bony pale hands touching her small but attractive boobs and stroking her glamorously dark curls.

Who else was he kissing while he wasn't kissing me? Those sophomores he sometimes ate lunch with? Girls from the cross-country team? Seniors he knew from the November Week retreat? He could be kissing girls all over the Tate Universe without me knowing anything about it.

I came out of the bathroom stall where I'd flushed the note, splashed some water on my face and put on red lipstick.

Then I wiped it off again.

Noel had been kissing Ariel Olivieri.

Kissing.

Ariel.

Ag.

I felt shattered.

Except, how could I be shattered? We weren't together. We would never be together, because of Nora liking him. We had barely spoken to one another since the term started.

Get over it, I told myself. You're not allowed to be shattered.

He's your Chem partner. You're his bodyguard.

Nothing more.

●

Noel was waiting for me outside the lab. "Did you get my note?" he asked.

I nodded.

"Did you eat it?"

I nodded.

"You did not."

I patted my stomach.

"Tell me you did not. Now I'm getting worried."

"I needed a snack to tide me over till lunch," I told him. "My mother made me drink kale-apple juice for breakfast. She said I'd feel invigorated and my electrolytes would be balanced."

"Did it work?"

I shrugged. "Well, I followed that with a venti vanilla latte. Meghan and I got drive-through Starbucks."

Noel wrinkled his forehead. "That can't be a good mix."

"No. So thanks for the piece of paper. It helped settle my stomach."

We went into the classroom and took seats at our usual lab table. Ariel and Katarina were next to us. Neanderthals Josh and Darcy on the other side. Noel leaned in and whispered: "Stay close. The enemy is at hand."

I liked the feeling of his breath in my ear. "That Fruit Roll-Up better be apricot," I told him sharply. "I'm not dealing with this situation for anything less than apricot."

Fleischman clapped his hands loudly. His comb-over flopped endearingly in the wrong direction. "Emulsions!" he yelled. "An emulsion is a stable mixture of two things that do not normally mix. Oil and vinegar are usually separate, yes? Put them both in a jar, and the oil stays on top and the vinegar on the bottom. Mix them together, and they will separate themselves. But it's possible to add an emulsifier, perhaps a little mustard or egg yolk, mix

vigorously, and create a stable mixture: salad dressing!
Now, name me another emulsion you encounter in your
kitchen."

No one raised their hands.

"Emulsions? People?"

No response.

"Okay, then I'll call on someone. Oliver! Name an
emulsion."

I hadn't done the reading. "Um. There's emulsion on
film?"

"In your kitchen, Oliver!" boomed Fleischman. "Do
you have film in your kitchen?"

"Actually, we do keep film in the fridge," I said. "My
dad has yet to cross over to digital."

Noel laughed. "Pudding," he said, distracting
Fleischman from his attack.

Fleischman jumped with happiness. "Pudding! Exactly! A pudding is a stiffened emulsion! And how about
mayonnaise?"

He went on for a long time about droplets of oil, agita-
tion and protein molecules. He also revealed himself to be
a mayonnaise enthusiast, waxing on about hollandaise,
aioli and other sauces that are basically glorified mayo.

"Wait," Katarina interrupted. "Go back one step.
There's egg in mayonnaise?"

"Duh," said Noel.

"Yes," said Fleischman. "It was in the reading. And it's
on the ingredient list." He bounded over to the table at the
front of the room, secured a jar of Hellmann's and handed
it to Katarina.

"Ugh!" she said, shaking her head. "I don't like eggs."

"Do you like mayonnaise?" asked Fleischman.

"I thought I did."

"Then you like eggs! Now, I want each of you to choose a whisk, two eggs, some vinegar, a timer and a beaker of olive oil. Bowls, measuring cups and salt shakers are already on your tables."

Ariel stood to go get her ingredients, but instead of heading directly to the front of the room she walked over to Noel and stood six inches closer to him than was necessary.

"Some of our whisks have many strands," Fleischman announced. "Some have few. I want you to count the strands on your whisks, people, then compare with your neighbors the length of time it takes to create your emulsions. The recipe is on the board!"

Ariel tossed her hair. "Hi, Ruby. Hi, Noel. How's it going?"

"Spankin'," I told her. "Spankin' with a side of ennui."

"Fine," said Noel.

"Did you make any New Year's resolutions, Ruby?" she asked, staring at Noel.

Yeah, I thought.

I resolved to keep my hands off Noel. But I didn't know that doing so would mean he'd take up with *you*.

"I canceled all my catalog subscriptions and gave up bottled water," I said instead.[3]

---

[3] *Canceling catalogs and giving up bottled water:* Actually, kind of true. My mother made those environmental resolutions for our entire family and forced Dad and me to promise we wouldn't secretly buy water or resubscribe to the

"Oh, wow. What a good person you turned out to be," Ariel said.

"Thanks," I muttered.[4]

She adjusted the hem of her T-shirt. "I resolved to broaden my musical horizons."

"That's cool," I said. Noel was slouching in his chair and staring at our salt shaker.

"Like I'm getting into punk and indie rock now," Ariel went on. "Not just listening to what comes on the radio. Hey, do either of you know anything about music? I could use some help knowing what to buy that's, you know, off the beaten track."

She didn't mean me.

"All my friends are useless on the subject," she continued.

Noel raised his eyebrows at me, as if to say, Will you get her out of here?

I stood. "Come on, Ariel," I said, as cheerily as possible, linking my arm through hers. She jerked in surprise but didn't pull away. "Let's get our eggs."

Ariel was compliant. "Bye, Noel!" she called as we walked to the front of the room.

He didn't answer.

Abercrombie catalog, tempting as that might be. And lest you wonder about my heavy Starbucks consumption, Mom bought me and Meghan venti-size reusable thermos cups.

[4] What a good person I turned out to be? *Turned out to be?* It sounds like a compliment on the surface, but actually what Ariel meant was: "All your life you've been a selfish person, and more recently you've been a roly-poly slut, so it never occurred to me you might do anything of value in the world."

We got our eggs, mixed them with olive oil, lemon juice and salt. Made emulsions. Generated hypotheses about whisks. Listened to Fleischman talk about emulsifiers and what they did and how they did it.

All through class, whenever Ariel said anything to Noel, I answered.

It happened a lot.

Ariel and I had a number of awkward, cheerful conversations.

She didn't like me, though, so eventually she gave up. Score one for the bodyguard.

At the end of class, Fleischman offered us all Tupperware so we could take our mayonnaise home and eat it on sandwiches. "It's an edible experiment, people!" he called as one hundred percent of us left the room without mayo. "Think about it. Now you know the chemical process behind some of your favorite everyday foods!"

In the hallway, Noel grabbed my hand as we strolled toward the refectory. "Thanks," he said. "You were completely excellent back there."

His hand was warm, and part of me wanted nothing more than to hold it, but I shook it off. "I'm not cut out for bodyguarding," I said.

"Don't sell yourself short. You did brilliantly."

"Maybe," I said. "But it makes me ill."

"Talking to Ariel? Come on, she's not that bad."

"It makes me ill that I'm helping you be a jerk to her," I told Noel. "Can't you see she likes you?"

His mouth hardened into a thin line. "That's what you're upset about?"

"Yes," I lied. I mean, I *was* upset about helping him be a jerk, but I was upset about a lot more than that. "If you kissed Ariel, or whatever, you should be nice to her."

He shook his head. "You want me to be nice to Ariel?"

I couldn't tell him how I actually felt, because how I actually felt was a ginormous mess.

1. I was mad at Noel for kissing Ariel.
2. I was mad at myself for being mad. Because I had no right to be mad.
3. I was mad he'd even *told* me about kissing Ariel, like I was a girl he had never been romantically interested in. Like I was only a friend and wouldn't care in the slightest.
4. If he did have to tell me about kissing Ariel, I was mad he didn't tell me what exactly happened. "Physical contact" is vague. No girl would ever just say "physical contact."
5. He probably did do more than kiss Ariel. Because if it was just a kiss, he would have said just a kiss. And more than a kiss on a first encounter? That meant he must have been really into it—even if now he's saying he wasn't.
6. I was mad that Noel asked me to bodyguard him from Ariel, because I didn't like her and she didn't like me and I had to talk to her all through Chem.
7. I was mad he asked me because he shouldn't have put me in the middle when I had nothing to do with his scamming adventures.
8. I was mad because he was being a jerk to her and now I was a part of it.

9. I was mad at myself that I didn't say no when he asked me to be a bodyguard.
10. I was mad at Ariel for moving in on Noel.
11. I was mad at myself for being mad at Ariel, who had a perfect right to express interest in a single guy who after all had been making out with her only a few days ago.

All this was going on in my head as we walked toward the refectory, and I was trying to figure out what to say, because of course I actually wanted Noel to have nothing to do with Ariel ever again—but that would have been a ridiculous thing to say because that was what he was proposing to do in the first place—and so if I said *that*, it would make no sense whatsoever that I was mad.

Then Jackson Clarke walked by, jeans low on his hips, ratty red sweater with the holes in the elbows, hair scrunched down by a knit cap—he walked by and hip-checked me. "Hey there, Ruby, nice anchor coat."

And I couldn't answer Jackson, and I couldn't answer Noel, and I started to feel that panicky feeling, the feeling like I couldn't breathe and was going to die and my heart was ratcheting around in my chest like it wanted to burst out of my puny rib cage and maybe I would just keel over right now and die in the middle of the path, and then Noel and /or Jackson and preferably both of them would realize my tragic beauty and complete excellence and go on to be better men because inspired by my memory.[5]

57

---

[5] Movies in which the woman dies and thereby helps the hero to realize his full manly potential in the world, only, of course, bad luck for her because she's

Ag.

No air.

Pain.

Beating chest.

This awful panic feeling was the whole reason I had to start going to the shrink in the first place, but I'd thought that now these attack things were *over* and I'd never have to feel this way again—but this was my stupid life, so apparently not.

"I gotta sit down," I said to Noel.

There was nowhere to sit.

I plonked down in the middle of the path.

The muddy path, in my white coat with brown anchors.

There was no air anywhere. My chest hurt.

I tried to remember what Doctor Z said. Picture a meadow full of flowers. Breathe slowly. In through the nose. Out through the mouth.

In through the nose. Out through the mouth.

You are outdoors, Ruby, I told myself. There is enough air here for you to breathe.

You are young and healthy. You are not having a heart attack.

---

dead: *Moulin Rouge; Braveheart; City of Angels/Wings of Desire* (same plot, different films); *Dangerous Liaisons; Sweeney Todd* (well, he only *thinks* she's dead and he becomes a total psycho, but still); *A Walk to Remember; The Prestige; Casino Royale* (the Daniel Craig one, not the Woody Allen one); *Harold and Maude; Love Story;* and *Finding Neverland.* So you see where I got this idea. It's everywhere! Despite being kinda sick.

"Roo, what are you doing?" Noel asked. He knew I had the panic things. He'd just never seen me have one.

"I'm sitting down," I said. The brick pathway was cold.

"Because you want me to be nice to Ariel?" Noel asked.

I shook my head.

"Are you sick?"

I shook my head again.

Jackson had stopped on his way to class. Now he bent over me. "You don't look good," he told me.

Thanks a lot.

"She's all gray and clammy," Jackson said to Noel. "She looks awful, don't you think?"

If I had to be neurotic, couldn't I turn glamorously pale and faint into someone's arms and make him want to rescue me? Did I have to hyperventilate in an ugly coat and sit in the mud?

In through the nose. Out though the mouth.

There is enough air here for you to breathe.

You are not having a heart attack.

"What's happening?" It was Nora's voice. I saw her tartan sneakers in front of me.

"Roo looks really bad," Jackson repeated.

"She sat down on the path," said Noel.

"Leave her with me, you guys," Nora said, ever practical.

They didn't go.

"I'm serious. She'll be okay. The two of you go on to class. Nothing to see here," Nora told them.

"All right, if you're sure," said Jackson.

"I should get to English," said Noel. "Roo, are you gonna be okay?"

I couldn't answer.

"She's going to be fine," said Nora. "Please, leave."

And so they did. Noel's steel-toed combat boots and Jackson's blue and orange Pumas walked off in the direction of the main building.

Nora, wonderful Nora, rummaged in her backpack and pulled out a Tate Prep hoodie. "Lift up your butt," she said.

I did, and she scooted the hoodie under me, then sat down next to me on the little that was left of it, patting my arm.

We just existed there for a minute or two, not saying anything. I started to feel like I had enough air. "Don't you have class?" I asked finally.

"I have fifth-period lunch with you, silly."

Oh, yeah.

I pulled a bit of soggy grass out from between the bricks. "Jackson kept saying I looked awful."

"What do you care?"

"I don't. But I'd still rather I looked gorgeous."

"You are gorgeous," Nora said. "He's a poohead."

"I know."

"I know you know."

"What happened just now?" she asked me.

"Oh, you know. Mental breakdown. Panic thing. My usual insanity," I told her.

"I mean, what happened that made you panic?" she pushed.

I shook my head. She was a wonderful friend.

She was sitting on the path with me.

She liked Noel.

I couldn't tell her.

7.

I Receive a Frog Laden with Meaning

Hi, Roo,

>You okay? I was concerned your anchor coat might be stained.
>Here is a frog for ya, to cheer you up.
>—Jackson

—on his signature pale green narrow-ruled paper, folded in quarters, with a funny drawing of a frog on the outside; found in my mail cubby, end of the day Wednesday.

back when we started going out, Jackson used to leave little ceramic frogs in my mail cubby each week. Long story.

After those stopped, he still used to leave notes almost every day, funny things about nothing much—what he'd had for dinner, a stupid thing Dempsey had said, how he'd thought of me when something came on the television. But I used to wish for more frogs. They were a symbol of how happy we were together, and as things got complicated, as things got ugly, I hated all the frogless days and wished the frogs would return.

Now here was another frog, after all that time. Sitting in my mail cubby when I swung by after History of Europe.

Was it an innocuous frog? As in, Ruby likes frogs, Ruby was upset today, I'll cheer her up with a completely innocent and free-from-connotations frog?

Or was is a Frog Laden with Meaning?

And if it was a Frog Laden with Meaning, what did it mean?

1. I love you again, take me back.
2. I feel nostalgia for when I loved you, but I don't love you.
3. I want to see if I can make you love me again, because I like to be adored, but not because I love you.
4. I want Kim to look in your mail cubby and see that I gave you a frog and go wild with jealousy.
5. I like jerking you around because you're such a sucker and you can't seem to quit me.

I knew I should throw it in the trash and never think about it again, but I couldn't.

●

During lunch on Thursday, Operation Sophomore Love was swinging as Nora and I came out of the serving line with our trays. There was Meghan, lip gloss shining, gray chamois shirt unbuttoned to show cleavage, standing at the head of a table full of sophomore boys and balancing her lunch tray against her hip.

"You do not!" she was saying.

"True story," said a tall one with braces on his teeth.

"Then maybe I should go out for crew this year instead of tennis," Meghan said. "Do you think I should?"

"Without a doubt." A different sophomore, Italian-looking, with pale brown skin and thick eyelashes, was trying to get her attention.

"You'd be great at it," said the one with braces.

Meghan touched her hair. "There are my friends," she said. "See you boys later!"

"See you boys later?" I muttered to Nora before Meghan reached us. "Who on earth says 'See you boys later'? She sounds like a film from 1954."

"Only to you," said Nora. "No one else watches films from 1954. The rest of us are watching movies in first run."

I threw a raisin at her.

"How's the Operation going?" I asked Meghan as she sat down with her tray.

She shrugged. "They're hard to tell apart, that's my biggest obstacle," she said. "One is Mark, one is Mike, one is Dave and one is Dan. If any of them turns out to have a two-syllable name, that's the one I'll have to pick."

I looked over. "Which is the one with the eyelashes?"

"Mike or Mark, but I don't know which."

"He's pretty cute."

"Yeah, but there's another guy who looks a lot like

him who just left. So this guy could be Dan, maybe. Oh, there's one of them called Don as well."

"I know that guy. Don who's on the basketball team?" Nora said. "Didn't we used to recognize these people from playing in the yard in elementary school?"

Meghan giggled. "I'm sure we did, but that was before puberty. They look different now."

"Ugh," I said. "I hate that word."

"What word, *puberty*?" Meghan said.

"My health is delicate," I told her. "Please don't say it again or I may chunder."

"What am I supposed to say, then?" said Meghan.

"Adolescence?" put in Nora.

"That's hardly better," I told them. "Say . . . um . . . mocha latte."

"Mocha latte?" Nora cracked up. "What are you talking about?"

"Mocha latte sounds nice, doesn't it? Mocha latte does not conjure images of acne and body odor and pubic hair that we don't need to be thinking about any more than necessary. Mocha latte sounds tasty."

"Okay," said Meghan. "So they look a lot different after mocha latte than they did in elementary."

"I love it!" said Nora. "Mocha latte has come upon the sophomore boys and they're starting to look good to us."

"Hooray for mocha latte!" cried Meghan.

"Listen," said Nora. "If I asked Noel to go skiing this weekend, to this house party at my family's mountain place, would you guys go? You know, to make it like a group thing?" She twisted a piece of her hair. "I'm allowed to invite friends, and this way it won't be so obvious I really want *him* to go."

"I'm there," said Meghan. "You'll be out of *Noboyfriend* by Monday."

"No thanks," I said.

"Why?" Nora looked at me, surprised.

"I don't ski. You know that." I hadn't even seen Noel since the whole bodyguarding panic attack debacle yesterday. I didn't think I could stand to spend the weekend watching Nora flirt with him on the ski lift.

"You can use my old Dynastars," said Nora. "The ones I used back when I was your height."

"I still won't be able to *actually ski*."

"Oh, come anyway. You can learn!" said Nora. "You can go on the bunny hill."

"I don't have a ski jacket."

"Oh, I have three," said Meghan. "I have goggles, I have everything. We'll set you up."

"My parents hired a chef for the weekend," said Nora, "so the food'll be good."

"Can I explain something?" I said. "One: I hate being cold. Two: I don't ski. Three: I hate sports with lots of gear. Four: I don't even know what a bunny hill is. Five: People die skiing. Six: I don't want to be one of them."

"You play goalie," said Nora. "You're not really scared of gear."

"And you're not going to die on the bunny hill," said Meghan. "Three-year-olds can ski the bunny hill."

"Seven: I do not want to spend the day with a bunch of three-year-olds who ski better than me."

"There's a shelf full of mystery novels people have left at our house over the years," said Nora. "You can hang out by the fireplace."

She knew me very well.

"There's a flat-screen TV with DVD, plus a minifridge in the den," Nora coaxed.

"I have to work at the zoo," I told her. "The penguins and the pygmy goats won't know what to do without me." I took a deep breath and tried to be a good friend. "But it's great you're inviting Noel," I lied. "And you know what you should do in the mornings?"

"What?"

"You should bake those cinnamon buns," I said.

"Really?"

"Yes. Because even though the way to a guy's heart is through his–"

"Nether regions!" cried Nora. This was an old joke.

"–there is no way romancing the stomach can hurt."

"Hm," she said. "I would never have thought of that."

"Those buns are some serious deliciousness," I told her. "And Noel is the kind of guy who would appreciate them."

Nora hugged me. "Thanks, Roo."

I felt slightly sick, but I smiled.

8

I Correspond with a Pygmy Goat

Dear Robespierre,

I often wonder if you mind being a pygmy goat. Does it make you feel inadequate next to the larger goats? Or do you feel supercute and adorable?

Also, do you understand English?

And do you, as a boy pygmy goat, ever worry about the girl pygmy goats? Do you feel conflicted and wonder whether you're most fond of Imelda or Mata Hari? Or do you, perhaps, feel goatly affection for some full-size specimen like Anne Boleyn, and wish she would notice your pygmy charms?

Please reply as soon as possible.

Fondly,

Ruby Oliver

(the one with zebra-stripe glasses who scratches your ears the way you like)

—written by me on Woodland Park Zoo stationery and placed in a bright blue box labeled "Write to Our Farm Animals!"

after school the next day Meghan dropped me at the Woodland Park Zoo. My internship there had started first term junior year, and now I was scheduled for Friday afternoons and Saturday days. It didn't pay much, but I liked it. Plus, I needed the money. My parents made me pay for a percentage of the gas we used in the Honda, and I owed them for a school retreat I went on in November.

At the zoo, my job was to give a short lecture during the Humboldt penguin feeding and help out in the Family Farm. I had gotten quite friendly with the goats and llamas. I fed them little food pellets and stroked their soft, hairy necks and told them how good-looking they were. I didn't mind if they chewed my sleeves or slobbered on me. I was always glad to see them.

Sometimes my job was to muck out stalls (only for farm animals, not for anything wild), and sometimes I wore a stupid-looking button that said "Ask me." Then school groups and inquiring kids could pump me for information about the names of the llamas (Laverne and Shirley) or the way to work the food dispensers so you could feed the goats.

Doctor Z thought all this was good for my mental

health. Working with animals got my mind off the badness of life in the Tate Universe and prevented me from using all my free time fixating on things like

1. Why Noel made out with Ariel if he didn't like her, or
2. Whether Noel would start liking Nora on the ski weekend, or
3. Whether it was wrong to encourage Nora to win Noel's heart with cinnamon buns when I didn't really mean it, or
4. Why the suddenly single Jackson was telling me I looked bad and then drawing me a Frog Laden with Meaning, or
5. How insane I must be to scope Mr. Wallace's chest hair when he was trying to talk to me about sports and literature.

When I got to the zoo, Anya, the intern supervisor, waved to me from her office as I signed in. "Hope you had a good vacation, Ruby," she said, shrugging on her coat. "I'll walk you halfway to the Farm, if you don't mind."

Anya was freckled and burly, with braces on her teeth even though she was maybe thirty-five years old. I liked her fine, although she had an air of never, ever leaving the zoo.

As we walked, Anya told me the news about the Family Farm creatures. For example, there was now a box where kids could write notes to the farm animals, plus a box of zoo stationery and minipencils. I was supposed to encourage patrons to write to their favorite goat, pig, llama, whatever. Robespierre, one of the pygmy goats, had had a hoof infection that was being treated, so I had to keep an eye out and inform someone if I noticed a limp or anything else unusual. The pig named Lizzie Borden was in a different pen than she used to be.[1] And so on.

I pinned on my "Ask me" button and said goodbye to Anya. The next hour I spent patting the goats and the pig, writing a note to Robespierre and pretty much killing time until a huge after-school group came into the Family Farm yelling and annoying the llamas. The kids were pelting me with questions and then not listening to the answers, and while I was busy with them this dad arrived with a toddler. The dad seemed kinda drunk, but I didn't pay him any attention because the school group was milling around and jostling each other to pet Lizzie Borden.

In the Family Farm area, the animals live in pens. The fences are low—you can reach right over them. While I was at the other end of the enclosure, surrounded by after-schoolers, this drunk dad lifted his two-year-old and stuck her on Robespierre's back for a ride. Robespierre bucked. The little girl fell off.

All that happened in about two seconds. "Excuse me," I said to the crowd of six-year-olds around the pig, and ran over to the goat pen. The toddler stood up, whimpering.

---

[1] Aside from Laverne and Shirley, most of the Family Farm animals are named after criminals, which is a problem when you are asked to explain their origins to a camp group of six-year-olds. Robespierre, I learned in History of Europe, was a leader of the French Revolution who killed ginormous numbers of people during the Reign of Terror. Lizzie Borden was famous for killing her parents with an axe.

She didn't look hurt. Her dad had forgotten about her because he was distracted trying to get food out of the dispenser, which is kind of hard to use, especially if you're *drunk*. Robespierre's infected foot must have hurt him, and he must have been scared, because he started chasing the toddler with his little pygmy horns lowered. The girl started running and screaming, and the drunk dad turned around. I leaped the fence, grabbed Robespierre by the neck and yelled at the dad to jump in and get his toddler.

He fell over as he was climbing in, cursing all the while, and stopped to brush the straw off his body before he picked up his crying kid. We all climbed out of the pen, and as we got our feet on the ground, he said, "You should have that thing put down, it's dangerous."

"What?" I couldn't believe what he was saying.

"It's not friendly. You saw that. It was chasing my kid!" he argued.

"Zoo guests aren't supposed to get in with the animals," I told him. "That's common knowledge. And I saw you put your kid on his back. What were you thinking? He's a tiny pygmy goat and his foot is infected. You hurt him."

"You!" The dad stuck his finger in my face and shook it. "You were not doing your job, which is to keep this family area safe and keep control of the animals!"

"I was too doing my job," I cried. "You weren't doing *your* job. You shouldn't be drunk and failing to watch your daughter. You shouldn't be sticking a little kid inside a pen."

"How old are you?" the man yelled. "How dare you talk to me like that?"

"You have no respect for the animals that live here," I yelled back. "You have no respect for your own kid and her safety. What kind of person does such a thing?"

"Your job is to watch the kids and keep the area safe!"

"You smell like beer!" I shouted. "I hope you're not driving your kid home."

I turned in disgust away from him—and then I saw Anya angrily striding toward us.

She gave me a harsh glare. "Sir, I'm the supervisor here. Is there any way I can assist you?" Her voice was exceedingly calm and polite.

"This worker is belligerent," he said, scooping up his crying daughter. "I asked for help with the feed machines and she started harassing me and my child."

"That's not true!" I said—but Anya held her hand up to silence me.

"I'm so sorry you had a negative experience here at the Woodland Park Zoo," she said soothingly. "Here." She dug in her pocket and pulled out a red lollipop. "Is it okay for her to have this?"

The man nodded and the toddler stuck out her hand for the candy.

"I apologize for the behavior of our intern here," Anya continued. "Please rest assured we will take the matter seriously."

"I want Mommy," said the toddler, sniffling.

Anya smiled. "Can I help you locate the rest of your family? Are they here at the zoo?"

"Yeah, that would be great, actually," said the man, wiping his forehead. "I have no idea where they got to."

Anya made an announcement over the zoo loud-speakers, which located the guy's wife, who had been over at the penguin exhibit with their older children.

As soon as they were gone and someone else arrived to wear the "Ask me" button at the Family Farm, Anya walked me back to her office. There, she demanded an explanation, but when I gave one, she didn't seem to listen to it. "You told him he smelled like beer, Ruby," she reprimanded. "There is no situation in which commenting on someone's smell is an appropriate response."

"But he—"

"No situation," she repeated.

Then I had to sit through a long lecture on how to treat zoo guests.

Then more lecture on how it was imperative that I keep an eye on the whole area even when there were school groups present.

Then guilt over how the zoo would now have to deal with news reporters questioning them and writing headlines like "Baby Mauled by Cranky Pygmy Goat."

And after all that, Anya fired me for negligence and abusive behavior toward patrons.

Really, she could have fired me without the lectures. Why remind me how to do my job if I'm not going to be working there, anymore?

Dear Robespierre,
    Goodbye, my goaty friend. I was fired from taking care of you because I was trying to take care of you.

I wonder if goats understand irony.

Please blow kisses to Laverne, Shirley, Kaczynski, Lizzie Borden and all the rest. I will miss you a lot and will come back to visit if they'll let me on the premises.
Your affectionate pal,
Ruby Oliver

I had a panic attack late that night. After I got out of Anya's office, after I snuck back to Family Farm to write my goodbye note to Robespierre, after I called my dad and asked him to pick me up early, after I made it through a dinner of sprouted-chickpea bread and something Mom called Sea-Veggie Pizza; after I had suffered through my mother saying Anya was an "unsympathetic troll" and my father saying he was sure that if I had another chance I'd "make different choices about how to handle a stressful situation"; after my father criticized my mother for the Anya-troll comment and after my mother yelled, "I'll call anyone a troll who acts like a troll! I say it like it is, Kevin! That's what I'm all about in this world. Saying it like it is, troll or no troll! You used to be able to handle it! You used to love that about me!"

After my mother burst into tears and ran into the bedroom, slamming the door shut, and after my father, without a word, dragged the box of sugary breakfast cereal from its hiding place underneath the kitchen sink and began to eat it, without milk; after Dad had washed the dishes and I had wiped the table, after he'd gone into the bedroom to make it up to my mother, after all that, when

I went to my room and was thinking, ironically, that I was handling the whole debacle with a reasonable degree of calm—after that, I had the panic attack.

I had lost my job.

Anya used to like me and now she thought I sucked.

I would miss Robespierre and Laverne and Shirley and the rest.

I would miss the smells of the zoo and the sound of the penguins as they dove into the water.

I would miss being good at something, good at relating to animals and speaking in public for the penguin feedings.

I had no money.

I had to earn money or I couldn't pay for gas.

If I couldn't pay for gas I couldn't use the car.

Also, I was living in the middle of my parents' marriage. No one ever says this about families, and maybe people who aren't only children don't even notice it, but half the time I feel like I'm this extra person watching them have a marriage. They fight, they kiss, they discuss the in-laws, they do projects, they take down the Christmas tree and reminisce about things I don't remember, they fight some more—and it's all this personal stuff that I really have no business witnessing, except I have nowhere else to go because I *live here.* I'm just trying to eat my dinner and instead I'm in the middle of this grown-up *relationship* that is complicated and disgustingly mushy and sometimes angry.

I know they're not getting divorced or anything, but when your parents argue it makes the whole universe seem like it's tipping, like everything could change if they got mad enough at each other, like the world isn't a safe place.

And of course, that's true, isn't it? The world is not a safe place.

All this I was worrying about on top of the job problem and the boy problems, and suddenly I couldn't breathe. There was no air in my room and my heart was so loud I felt sure my mom was going to pop in and say, "Roo, your father and I are having a serious conversation, could you please keep your heart down?"

No air.

No air.

I remembered this trick Doctor Z taught me, where you get a tennis ball and you toss it back and forth from one hand to the other, keeping your eyes on it. The concentration balances the two spazzing-out sides of your brain. Gasping, I left my room and went into my dad's greenhouse. I knew there were a couple of those hand-strengthening squeezy balls in there, because my dad uses them to de-stress.

The greenhouse smelled of dirt and flowers. I don't know what kind. There were some blooms and they weren't roses, that's all I know. I found one of the hand-strengtheners and sat on a plastic crate, tossing it back and forth. Back and forth. Just watching the ball and nothing else, until—after a bit—my breathing became normal and I looked up.

The southern deck of our houseboat looks out on the Hassinblads' northern deck, and I could see George Hassinblad through his window, cooking something in a pot on his stove and drinking root beer out of a bottle. The greenhouse felt calm and I could see the stars and there was stuff growing.

My heartbeat slowed. George Hassinblad's sporty little wife came in from a nighttime run and the two of them sat down to eat the soup he'd made. They laughed. George spilled soup on his lap and wiped it off with a dish towel.

My dad's old CD player is filthy with potting soil. On top of it sits a collection of CDs devoted entirely to nostalgic heavy metal. It's Hutch's fault. Ever since he became my dad's garden assistant, he's encouraged Kevin Oliver's musical tastes in directions that other people can only call unpleasant. He and Dad rock out whenever they're working in the greenhouse. I walked over and hit Play without looking at what was in the box.

Na na na NA na na na NA na.

Steven Tyler's demented squeal blasted through the greenhouse.

Na na na NA na na na NA na.

Aerosmith's "Walk This Way."

Retro metal isn't my thing, but I stood and danced like a maniac until the song was over.

9.

I Uncover the Secret Mental Health of Hair Bands

Hello there, Ruby,

You probably don't know this about me, but: my brownies have reached crazy ninja-good level.

Also, I am behind on community service hours.

If you want some help with the chubby thing, whatever it's called, let me know.

Finn

—found in my mail cubby, written on unlined white paper in lines of blue ink that slanted down toward the right corner of the page.

On Friday, Finn Murphy—soccer-team stud muffin and Kim's ex-boyfriend from before Jackson—Finn Murphy left me a note.

He had never written me a note. He was Kim's ex, but he'd liked me back in elementary school—therefore making him yet another boy I was supposed to stay far away from. Even now, months and months after they'd broken up, by talking to Finn I'd risk spoiling the delicate truce at which Kim and I had finally arrived just before winter break.

But hey, I needed bakers.

I got the note Monday afternoon, so Meghan and I went to the B&O Espresso after school. The B&O is a coffee bar a little ways off Broadway. It has spankin' cake. You can go in there and do your homework and drink lattes or espresso milk shakes and they never kick you out for being there too long. Finn was working the counter, like usual.

"Got your note," I said as Meghan and I walked in and plopped ourselves at the table nearest the register.

Finn blushed. Actually blushed, to the roots of his cropped sandy hair. He was wearing a white shirt with the sleeves rolled up and a black apron. He had the thin forearms and thick legs of a soccer player, big thoughtful eyes and the general look of someone who is good at skiing.

Why was he blushing?

Wasn't this about the ninja brownies?

It had better be about ninja brownies.

"I'll have a Valencia mocha," said Meghan.

"Same," I said. "And can I get the chocolate raspberry torte?" I had no business buying myself exotic tortes when I'd just lost my job, but the thing was calling to me in all its chocolaty deliciousness.

Finn wiped the counter in front of us and started making coffee drinks.

"You're our first boy," said Meghan.

"Don't bring gender into it," I said. "You're our first *anyone* besides me, Meghan and Nora. If you want, you can be a founding member of the inaugural Baby CHuBS."

Finn chuckled and shook his head. I wasn't sure if it meant yes, or no, or what.

"He's embarrassed!" yelled Meghan. "Finn, why are you embarrassed?"

"I'm not embarrassed," he answered, pouring milk. "I just feel bad because I was about to bail, and now here you guys are calling me a founding member."

"What? You can't bail on us," said Meghan. "We have your brownie pledge in writing."

Finn shrugged. "Well, I–"

I interrupted him: "You also can't describe ninja-good levels of brownies and then fail to follow through. How do we know you can even *make* ninja brownies?"

"I learned from the guys in the kitchen here," Finn said. "I started working the early-morning shift on weekends, so now I'm around when they're baking. I can do lemon bars too."

He put our lattes on the counter and gave us two extra-large pieces of chocolate raspberry torte. "It's on me, by the way," Finn said, gesturing at the cake.

"Really? I think I might love you." It was out of my mouth before I realized what I was saying.

Ag.

Cancel.

Erase.

Saying things like that to completely inappropriate boys who are not mine to say such things to is one of the reasons I have antagonized most of my former friends and am now a roly-poly.

How could I say that to Finn?

How stupid am I?

And of course, he blushed again.

Stop blushing, Finn! Stop it, stop it! I shoved a bite of torte into my mouth so I wouldn't talk anymore.

Meghan, who flirts with everyone and therefore has no need to go into mental gyrations any time something suggestive comes out of her mouth, saw it all in terms of Operation Sophomore Love. "Hey," she said, "maybe the other guys on the soccer team can bake too. How about some of the underclassmen?"

"Hardly." Finn laughed.

"What?" Meghan looked innocent. "They have a lot of free time. They don't have to worry about the SATs or anything. Don't you think you could get some of the JV players to contribute?"

Finn coughed on purpose. "The soccer team guys are not bakers."

"Why not?" Meghan asked, spooning a bit of foam from her mocha and licking it off in a way that would have made me hate her guts a year ago. "A guy who bakes is very attractive."

What the hell. It was all for charity, right? "Me too," I said. "Nothing is hotter than a guy who can feed me."

Finn stammered. He flushed. By the end of the conversation, he had promised to make ninja brownies *and* lemon bars, plus he swore he'd recruit the members of the soccer team for the manly baking project by convincing them that it would attract girls.

"This is going to change the whole social order at Tate," I said to Meghan as we left the B&O in the rain.

"It'll get us out of this state of *Noboyfriend,* if that's what you mean," she answered, unlocking the doors and climbing into the Jeep.

"No, I mean it'll change the antiquated sex roles that go on during bake sales," I said.

"Speak English."

"You know. Every year, girls bake. Boys eat. It's like the nineteenth century."

"I guess."

"That's why I never liked CHuBS that much in the first place. It was all girls in the kitchen. In fact, I bet you no boy has contributed to CHuBS, *ever.* And like Wallace said in American H and P last year, if you change one part of the pattern in a social system, the rest will have to shift in accordance."

Meghan said, "Finn was blushing the whole time we were in there. Did you notice?"

Yeah. I noticed.

Being Meghan, she didn't see how complicated it was that he was blushing at me and I'd noticed him blushing; and that I'd looked at his forearms with his shirtsleeves rolled up and that he gave me free cake. It was so, so complicated, because Finn used to be Kim's and I used to be Jackson's but Finn always looked at my legs, and today I'd said "Nothing is hotter than a guy who can feed me" like a complete slut and he kept blushing—it was all so complicated, my heart started pounding.

I didn't want to have a panic attack. This was the third one in like a week.

Breathe, Ruby, breathe, I said to myself.

It doesn't have to happen. You are in charge of yourself.

But there wasn't any air in the car.

Stop, heart, slow down, I thought. There is nothing to spaz out about.

The only thing that's happening is that a boy you've known since kindergarten is helping with your bake sale.

Breathe.

I reached out and turned the radio on, then hit the button for K-ROCK. Guns N' Roses' "Paradise City" banged through the Jeep's speaker system. Retro metal. I pushed the volume up and closed my eyes.

There. With Guns N' Roses on, I couldn't think about anything. Didn't panic. Just turned off my brain until Meghan said, "You know I love you, but Hutch has totally warped your musical taste," and shoved a Rihanna CD into the stereo.

Nora, Meghan and Noel were all skiing that weekend, so I job-hunted all day Saturday, bringing photocopies of my sucky résumé to shops along University Ave and calling places listed in the newspaper: a tanning salon, the Jamba Juice in Bellevue Square, a telemarketing company that was looking for people to make cold calls about mattresses.

Sunday my dad and Hutch were pruning early-flowering rhododendrons and discussing various techniques for a gardening article my dad was writing for the *Seattle Post-Intelligencer*. Hutch and I drilled each other for our Monday French quiz and the three of us went out and got Chinese food for lunch while my mom was at her yoga class.

Hutch asked me about the whole zoo debacle, and when I explained what happened he said he was boycotting the zoo to protest my losing my job.

"Thanks," I told him. "But when was the last time you actually *went* to the zoo?"

"Sixth grade," he admitted, shoveling a piece of garlic broccoli into his mouth.

"So you average once every five years or so?" I asked. He nodded.

"Your support means a lot," I said. "I'm sure the zoo will take your protest extremely seriously."

"Never let it be said I didn't do my part," he said, reaching across me to snag the lo mein. "I defend your right to tell people how they smell, any day of the week."

He smelled of garden dirt, soy sauce and a bit of BO, but I didn't say anything.

When we got home, I called Nora to find out how Operation Ski Bunny Romance was going, but she didn't pick up.

Neither did Meghan.

So I did my Am Lit homework.

●

Monday in Chem we curdled milk by adding vinegar and then squeezing it out in pieces of cheesecloth. In the middle of the disgustingness, I couldn't resist asking Noel, "How was Crystal Mountain?"

"Excellent."

What did he mean, excellent? Did he mean that he and Nora had fallen in love? Or did he mean there was nice powdery snow?

"What did you do?" I asked.

"Meghan's way better than me or Nora, so she went off with Gideon and some friends of his to ski Otto Bahn. Nora and I are well matched, so we stuck to Kelly's Gap Road and stuff like that."

I was annoyed. Why did skiers always talk about slopes like nonskiers had any idea what they were on about? And had he really skied with Nora all weekend? Riding on those chairlifty things, just the two of them, looking out at beautiful scenery?

Ag.

Or rather, Oh, I'm so happy for Nora.

Why didn't being a good friend come naturally to me? Fleischman started babbling about casein and positively charged H^+ ions and a lot of other boring stuff. I dried my hands when he told me to and tried to take notes on the lecture, but none of it was sticking with me.

"I mean, what did you do besides ski?" I finally asked Noel, when Fleischman was done talking and we were all supposed to be coming to the front of the room to taste various cheeses and think about what we'd learned in terms of their chemical makeup. "Roquefort!" Fleischman was shouting. "Epoisses! That one is stinky, watch out! Did you know raw-milk cheeses are illegal in the US of A? Yes, people! Can anyone explain why? Did anyone do the reading on pasteurization?"

I *had* done the reading, but I was more interested in what Noel was going to say than in gaining points with Fleischman.

Noel shrugged. "Nora brought some movies and we watched them."

"And?"

Noel put some Epoisses in his mouth and made a slight face. "She made these cinnamon swirl things on Sunday morning. They were seriously good."

Nora had taken my advice.

I wished she hadn't.

"She made blueberry muffins too," Noel added. "Amazing."

"I wasn't asking for the Nora report," I snapped.

He looked puzzled. "You asked about the weekend."

"So?"

"So, I was just telling you."

"Back to your places, people!" Mr. Fleischman called,

his comb-over flopping off his head. He sat us down and began to discuss the difference in curd-granule junctions between brick cheese and Cheddar, and explaining that next week we would be looking at the junctions under microscopes.

Noel bent over his notebook seriously. I bent over mine. We didn't say anything more.

When class is over, I told myself, I'm going to walk out without giving him another glance.

It's not like Noel is anything to me.

He was making out with Ariel last week.

He can fall for Nora and her cinnamon buns. I'll be nothing but happy for them.

I don't care.

Fleischman finished talking, and immediately I bent down to pick up my backpack. When I stood up, ready to dodge Noel so as not to have to continue our conversation, he was already gone.

●

"I think retro metal is maybe a cure for panic disorders," I told Doctor Z the next day.

She popped a square of Nicorette. "Ruby."

"Yes?"

"You don't have a panic disorder."

I crossed my legs and picked at the fraying knee of my jeans.

"You know that, don't you?" repeated Doctor Z.

"Yes."

"Three attacks in one week don't–"

"Two attacks were in one day!" I interrupted.

"Fine. They're still not enough to constitute a disorder. It's an important part of our therapy that we keep you thinking rationally about your panic attacks. Because it is when people begin to fear them and avoid situations because of possible triggers that a disorder can emerge."

I knew all about that. "I am thinking rationally," I told her. "I'm telling you I think the cure is retro metal."

"Tell me about it."

"Retro metal is how Hutch survived years of roly-poly-ness without becoming hospitalized for mental stress. He just rocks out on a regular basis to the likes of Poison or Van Halen or whatever, and it keeps him from going insane. It's the secret mental health of hair bands."

A smile played at the corner of her mouth. "What's a hair band?"

"You know, those bands with ginormous teased-up hair they flip around while they play guitar," I explained. I knew I was wasting my therapy hour, but I kept going: "Retro metal is how my father manages to live with my supercontrolling mother. I expect the metal has to have some kind of a beat. Like AC/DC works, Aerosmith works, but not Metallica or any other speed metal."

Doctor Z shook her head gently.

"You doubt me," I said, "but I'm telling you, this theory is golden. You could write a book on the subject and become famous."

"Well," she conceded, "music can be an excellent stress release."

"I'm saying, music that I don't even like. Music that by most objective standards actually sucks. Who would imagine it could be therapeutic?'

"Ruby."

"What?"

She didn't say anything. I hate it when she does that. I didn't say anything back.

But I hated sitting there in silence, too. "It's so passive-aggressive when you say my name and then don't say anything else," I finally told her.

Nothing from Doctor Z.

"I know you don't want to hear my theory of retro metal," I went on. "I know you think it's a front to avoid talking about something real."

Silence again.

"No doubt you want me to talk about *why* I had the panic attacks."

Nothing.

"Or explain more about what happened beforehand."

More nothing.

"Did you know Jackson said I looked bad when I had the panic thing on the path at school?" I said. "It kills me that he said I looked bad. He even told *Noel* I looked bad."

Doctor Z chewed her Nicorette thoughtfully.

"You're thinking about how I'm talking about Jackson again, aren't you?" I said. "Because I haven't even told you about the Frog Laden with Meaning. If I were still obsessed with Jackson, that would have been like, the first thing I mentioned when I got in here. The Frog Laden with Meaning."

"Actually . . . ," Doctor Z said.

But I went on: "Did I tell you Nora invited Noel skiing? Nothing happened between them, she told me, but they got to know each other much better and she's optimistic. Plus she baked him cinnamon buns and I know for a fact he was impressed. Nora is like a role model for going after what you want, don't you think? I should try to be more like her. I'm sure all my mental problems would be better if I embarked on the Imitate Nora Van Deusen Program for a Happier Mocha Latte (aka adolescence)."

"Actually," repeated Doctor Z, with only a slight sigh, "I was thinking that since we're coming up against some resistance on your part to engaging with me on topics of substance, maybe it's time for you to make a treasure map."

"A what?"

"A treasure map. Our time is over for today, but it would be useful for you to do at home, to bring in next week. It's a project."

I gave her a doubtful look.

"It's a treasure map because it's a concrete imagining of something you want for yourself in life," explained Doctor Z. "In this case, positive relationships with your peer group. But the map will make things more specific."

"I'm supposed to draw a map of positive peer-group relationships?" I stood and heaved my bag over my shoulder.

"Like a friendship collage," said Doctor Z. "You're showing yourself what you want your social life to look like. You can use photographs, words, paint, fabric, any kind of mixed media. Include activities you'd like to do with your friends, images that illustrate how you feel about your peers and possibly about your romantic prospects."

She sounded like she was reciting something from a textbook of shrinky ideas, and I wondered if she'd looked up treasure mapping in her secret *Instruction Manual for the Care and Treatment of Annoying Teenagers* before I arrived for my appointment.

"Whatever," I told her.

"Give it a try," Doctor Z said, and she had this hopeful, earnest look in her eyes that made me think she really, truly did want to help me be a normal person.

"Yeah, okay," I told her. "I'll get out my glue stick."

•

Both my parents were in the car waiting for me when I got out. They announced we were going to Judy Fu's Snappy Dragon for Chinese.

"How was Doctor Z?" asked my dad as I climbed into the backseat. He was behind the wheel of the Honda and there was garden dirt under his fingernails.

"Kevin, you're not supposed to ask her what happens in therapy," Mom said. The backseat was filled with plastic bags she wanted to reuse at the grocery store. I was squished in among them.

"I'm not asking what happened in therapy," Dad said. "I'm asking how Doctor Z is."

"She's fine," I told him. "She got a haircut."

"Did you learn anything interesting today?" he asked.

"It's not school, Kevin," my mother corrected him. "You can't ask her what she learned, because A, she didn't learn stuff and B, I already told you, you can't ask her what happened. It's supposed to be her business."

"Hello, I'm in the car." I said, scrunching grocery bags to make some noise in the backseat.

My mother ignored me. "Kevin, get on the freeway. It's shorter if you take I-Five."

"She could learn stuff," said Dad. "She's going through a growth process. It's different from school, but it's still learning."

"Learning that you *can't ask her about*. Do you think they have salad at Snappy Dragon?" Mom pulled out a compact and powdered her nose. "Because I'm going to need to eat raw there, you know."

"It's Chinese. Are you really expecting salad?"

"Eating raw is a commitment," Mom insisted. "It's no good if you cheat."

"You said okay to Snappy Dragon! I asked you!"

"Why are you so unsupportive of the raw-food way of life?"

Mom sulked for a few minutes and Dad drove. Finally, he said: "I don't see why Ruby wouldn't tell us what she learned. She doesn't have to give us details that feel private, she could share the insights she's gleaned, so as to help us relate to her better."

My mother sighed. "Take this exit."

"Is there anything else you want to share with us about therapy?" Dad asked me. "I hope you realize my ears are always open."

I don't know what came over me then. I was so mad at myself for wasting my therapy session—and honestly, I didn't think there was any way they'd believe me. "Doctor Z thinks I should get a dog," I answered.

"What? That's a strange prescription," my dad said.

"Actually," I continued, amused, "she thinks I should get a Great Dane."

"No way." My mother crossed her arms. "Kevin, left! Left right here!"

Dad turned obediently. "Doctor Z specified a dog breed?" he wanted to know.

"Yes," I lied. "But really she said any superlarge dog would do. It has to do with having a vessel for my psyche, and the vessel shouldn't be too small."

I thought for sure they were both going to start laughing any minute. But they didn't, so I went on. "It's supposed to work wonders for the ennui brought on by mocha latte."

"The what is supposed to do *what* for the *what* brought on by *what*?" my dad wanted to know.

"We're not getting a dog. *N-O* spells *no*," said my mother.

"I can spell," I reminded her.

"Tell Doctor Z she should check with us before putting ideas into your head," said Mom. "Juana has one of those dogs and it's a total menace."

10.

I Join Up with Granola Brothers

Hey hey Roo,
    I came by the bake sale table this morning but you weren't there.
    Jackson

    —written on his green-tinted narrow-ruled paper—but with *no frog;* no frog whatsoever.

I got this note after first period the next morning. I had an early meeting with my college counselor and had skipped sitting at the CHuBS recruiting table while Meghan and Nora gave out linzer cookies.

Why had Jackson come by the table?

What did he want?

And why was there no frog?

Had I expected a frog?

I wondered about it all morning, but I didn't see him until after sixth period, when I spotted him waiting to talk to Mr. Wallace as a group of seniors surged out of Contemporary Am Lit. He was wearing an old plaid shirt rolled above the elbows. His forearms were solid muscle from rowing crew.

"Hey." I tapped his shoulder.

"Ms. Roo to you, what's up?"

"You said something about the bake-sale table," I reminded him.

Mr. Wallace caught Jackson's eye. "I haven't forgotten about you, Clarke," he said. "Just give me one more minute here."

Jackson nodded at him and turned to me. "Oh, it was nothing important," he said. "I can tell you later."

I was annoyed. Why write me, then, if it was nothing important? It wasn't like we were friends. "Whatever," I said, turning to go—but he touched my arm.

"You're running the bake sale and it's happening on Parents' Day, is that what I hear?" he asked.

I nodded. "We're recruiting now."

Jackson flashed his grin. "Are there gonna be doughnuts?"

"Doughnuts are advanced," I said. "You deep-fry them. There's hot oil involved. Don't get your hopes up."

Jackson pulled a face. "Doughnuts would be so good, though, don't you think?"

"Maybe."

"You should get someone to make them," he said.

"In your dreams," I said, annoyed. "I gotta go to class."

"Yes, in my dreams!" he called after me as I went into Pre-Cal. "There are homemade doughnuts in my dreams!"

●

Even though I was lying about the Great Dane, it's true that I like animals more than people. That's a horrible thing to say, I know. It's also no doubt one of the reasons I need therapy. Wouldn't anyone with a modicum of sanity care more about the homeless, or battered women, or any kind of *person* who might end up in a shelter than she would about fuzzy kittens?

Yes, anyone with a modicum of sanity would. But to me, dogs and cats are innocent. Goats and llamas, too. They're never duplicitous, they're never bitchy, they're never untrue.[1] They never write you confusing notes, or stare at your boobs, or steal your boyfriend, or write things about you on the walls of the bathroom.

When you love an animal, you don't mind if it has bad breath, or chews on your hoodie, or chases a toddler because its foot is hurting. You just laugh at those things, and try to understand them, and appreciate the animal for who it is. It's not conditional love—but love between people seems like it nearly *always* is.

---

[1] Except llamas. Sometimes llamas *are* bitchy.

I got Archer to agree to switch our charity to Happy Paws, a no-kill "haven" that finds homes for abandoned dogs and cats, and Thursday afternoon I stayed late at school helping Meghan and Nora make posters for the Baby CHuBS recruiting table. Some were about Happy Paws, and the others offered a free baked good to anyone who signed up to contribute to the sale. The food would get the boys in, we figured.

"Guys will do almost anything for a chocolate chip cookie," said Nora. "I have a brother. Trust me, I know."

"Like what will they do?" I asked.

"Once I got Gideon and his friends to clean my room."

"Gideon cleaned your room?"

"He wouldn't do it now. He was like thirteen."

"What else?"

"He's loaned me his car. And his iPod. Stuff like that, just if I make him cookies."

Nora's brother, Gideon, is a freshman at Evergreen State College nearby in Olympia. It's one of those colleges where you make your own major. He's extremely hot in a messy, bohemian way, and I had a ginormous crush on him in sixth grade.

"Those must be magic cookies," put in Meghan. We had finished poster making and gone in the Jeep to the Pike Place Market to buy ingredients and baking paraphernalia. The Market is a big open-air craft and produce thing. Cobblestone streets. A view of Puget Sound. Fishmongers. Smells waft from the crumpet shop, Three

Girls Bakery and the dumpling place I don't know the name of.

"If Nora made the magic cookies now," Meghan mused aloud, "I could give a cookie to Mike and have him do my horizontal bidding."

I cracked up. "What about Mark, Dave, Dan and Don?"

"Whichever," said Meghan.

"You are a bad, bad woman," Nora said.

"You're the one making the magic cookies," said Meghan. "I'm just planning to use them to their fullest potential."

Nora looked at her. "I thought you wanted true love before Spring Fling."

Meghan shrugged. "Sure. But that was before I knew you could make magic cookies."

We entered a kitchen-supply store, and as we trolled the aisles, I wondered what I would do with magic cookies.

Make Kim and Cricket forgive me?

Make Noel fall in love with me?

Make Jackson want me?

I couldn't decide.

Nora didn't like any of the cookie cutters at Sur La Table. Archer wanted us to make rabbits and Easter egg shapes, but when we looked at them they were just so cutesy and Christian-centric we couldn't deal. So we gave up on baking supplies and followed Meghan over to the Birkenstock store. She's obsessed with those sandals, which is such a completely odd thing to be obsessed with, given that they are neither attractive nor practical. But there is no reasoning with that girl when it comes to footwear.[2]

Granola Brothers Footwear Emporium is in a corner of the Market devoted to stores selling Hmong tapestries, inexpensive cotton print blankets and silver jewelry. Inside the shop, Nora and I fingered batik shirts and tie-dyed dresses while Meghan debated earnestly between a pair of brown sandals and—another pair of brown sandals.

After a few minutes I noticed a sign on the counter saying HELP WANTED, so I asked the hippie man who was ponytailing around behind the counter what the job was.

"Working the register, selling Birks, restocking the sock wall"—there was a wall of colored socks—"and helping customers," he said. "We're a laid-back operation. Where have you worked before?"

I told him about the zoo internship and babysitting, leaving out the part about Robespierre and the drunk guy and being fired.

"And how do you feel about feet?" the guy asked.

Feet?

Ag. Who has strong feelings about feet?

"I think it's superimportant for people to have comfortable footwear," I told him. "I think happy feet make a happy person."

"Can you work Saturdays?" asked the guy. "Saturday is when it's really busy in here."

[2] Movies in which the romantic heroine sports Birkenstocks: none.

"Sure," I said.

"Come in tomorrow at nine. You'll get an hour of training on how to fit the shoes and work the register," he told me. "We open at ten. You'll need to wear Birks to work, but otherwise, consult your own personal style genie."

Suddenly, life was sweet.

I had a job!

Hello, use of the Honda!

Hello, no more debt to my parents!

Hello, cash flow!

And hello, Birkenstocks.

Hippie sandals and an anchor coat. My personal style genie was having a seriously horrible month.

11.

I Unleash the Powers of Magic Cookies

Thirteen Reasons Not to Look at Photos of Your Ex-Boyfriend

1. His smile lights up the picture. No one has a laugh like him.
2. He looks good without his shirt on. Really, phenomenally good.
3. Why did the two of you never get naked again? Why didn't you rip off his clothes the moment you had a chance? Because the way you are going now, in an apparently permanent state of *Noboyfriend*, that was the only opportunity you are ever going to get to touch a guy's naked chest. Which you really want to do before you die.
4. Look at the way he's got his arms around you in that photo. That was something real. No one could fake that. So how could he change from loving boyfriend into pod-robot[1]?

---

[1] *Pod-robot:* Looks like a person but has no personlike feelings. Possibly a human who has been taken over by an alien life-form, possibly just a spectacu-

5. Maybe he didn't change into a pod-robot. Maybe he still has buried feelings. After all, he did give you a Frog Laden with Meaning.

6. Remember how you two did that lollipop taste-test? Look, there he is making a funny face at the yucky grape flavor.

7. And remember how when you took that photo on the roof, he left you a note with mysterious instructions saying where to meet him and when, and then he kissed you up there and you looked at the view and took snapshots with the self-timer?

8. Remember, remember, remember . . .

9. What you had with this boy, for the time that it lasted—that is what you want out of love. The giddiness, the silliness, the comfort. That feeling is the whole reason to leave the state of *Noboyfriend*.

10. But will you ever be able to have that feeling with anyone but him?

11. Look, there he is with your ex–best friend. The two of them are holding pieces of sushi in their chopsticks and pointing at each other's food. Were they into each other then?

12. Were they holding hands under the table when you went to the bathroom? Were they laughing behind your back?

13. You will never know.

—from *The Girl Book*, written mid-February, junior year.

---

larly excellent robot. A relatively complete listing of movies with pod people, humanoid robots or something similar appears in a previous chronicle of the debacle that is my life, but here are a couple you really should watch if you have any pretensions to being a movie aficionado: *Westworld; The Terminator; The Stepford Wives* (1975 version).

Saturday I worked at Granola Brothers. The other sales-people were college students helping pay their way through the U. They were devoted to an earthy, tie-dye aesthetic and a diet that included the voluntary consumption of sprouts. Meghan had given me a hand-me-down pair of Birks, and I wore them with black tights and a vintage dress. Fletcher, my boss, trained me—and as I spent the day organizing socks and ringing up sales, I had to admit the shop was a friendly and cheerful place to work. I can't say I was interested in feet—everyone there talked about feet a lot—but being there and helping customers did keep my mind off my declining mental health, my precarious friendships and my parents' insanity.

When I got home I tried to make the treasure map Doctor Z wanted me to do, even though I didn't feel like it. (I doubted it would cure me of panic attacks, and I wanted to spend the evening eating take-out pizza and watching *Notting Hill* again. So romantic.)

But since I was afraid of the way Doctor Z would look at me if I went back on Tuesday without it, I started the map as soon as I was done writing my Chem lab. I cleared off my desk; found a big sheet of paper left over from Advanced Painting Elective last term, some watercolors, scissors and a glue stick—and dug out my pile of photographs of Jackson, from back when we were going out.

They were hard to look at.

They made me remember things I didn't want to remember.

What did I want from my "relationship" with him? That's what Doctor Z wanted to know in the treasure map.

Think of what you want from a situation, she was always saying, and then try to get it.

Except I didn't *have* a relationship with Jackson. I only *used* to have a relationship with Jackson. Then we broke up and spent a whole summer and first term junior year *not* having a relationship. Him being a pod-robot and me being a wreck. Then bit by bit, I got over him. Until he broke up with Kim and sent me the Frog Laden with Meaning.

What did I want?

Nothing.

No, that wasn't honest.

To be friends, nothing complicated. No frogs, no flirting.

No, that wasn't honest either. I wanted frogs! I wanted flirting. I wanted to have him love me again so I could humiliate him by rejecting him.

No. To have him love me again so I could prove to Kim and to myself that I was better than she was.

No. To have him love me again so I could experience true love.

No. Ag. No. There was not going to be true love with Jackson. He was a massive flirt and a cheater and generally bad news.

So what did I want?

Did I want him to love me?

Did I want to rip his clothes off?

Did I want redemption?

Revenge?

I painted the background of the treasure map with

a thin wash of blue watercolors, dark water fading into pale sky.

Jackson Clarke.

When the paint was dry enough, I pasted a picture of the two of us holding lollipops right in the center of the map. It was a picture of happiness. Romantic happiness.

Whether I wanted it with Jackson, whether I wanted it with Noel, whether I just wanted it in the abstract, I didn't know. But I wanted it.

Then I wrote: "Do not think about guys who have broken your heart six ways. It is mentally deranged to chase after heartbreak."

I looked through some old Tate directories and found a photo of Nora's brother, Gideon Van Deusen, looking bohemian, even in a school photo. I cut him out and pasted him on there. "Wanting guys you can't have is a recipe for unhappiness," I wrote, remembering sixth grade. "Do not fall for people who hardly know you exist."

Then I found a picture of Finn Murphy and wrote: "Liking a guy just because *he* likes *you*: Immature and pitiful? Or a smart interpersonal relationship strategy likely to result in true happiness?"

The note Noel had written me on the first day of school was in the front pocket of my backpack.

Say you'll be my partner true
In Chemistry, it's me and you.

I glued on a picture of Noel I'd taken during November week earlier that year. He was standing on a dock with a stretch of water behind him, doubled over laughing. Then I took a thick black marker and wrote those last two lines of his poem on the left side of the map.

That was what I wanted. Someone who wanted me. Someone who wanted a partner. Not a life partner, but a girlfriend. Someone who wanted there to be a "me and you."

Only, Noel didn't seem to want that anymore. If he ever had.

I mean, he wrote that note the morning after he had no doubt touched the pink sweatered boobs of Ariel Olivieri and pressed his lips against hers.

Ag.

Plus, he couldn't even figure out why I was mad about the bodyguarding thing. Plus plus, he had spent the weekend skiing with Nora, and he liked her cinnamon buns.

More ag.

I realized that as I'd been thinking, I'd written his name over and over in one corner of the map: "Noel. Noel. Noel. Noel."

I crossed it out. Instead, I wrote: "Someone who doesn't care if my hair looks stupid."

I wrote: "Something uncomplicated."

I wrote: "Something real."

Then I wrote: "But is it real if it's uncomplicated?"

I opened this history of cinema book Dad got me for Christmas and paged through to see if I could find an image to use on the map. Movie stills flipped by. Beautifully lit, gorgeous Caucasian people in black-and-white. Katharine Hepburn, Cary Grant, Barbara Stanwyck, Bette Davis. Then near the end of the book, in color. People looking more disheveled, perhaps, but still—no one's hair looked stupid. Faye Dunaway, Warren Beatty, Al Pacino, Diane Keaton, Gwyneth Paltrow.

There was kissing in those movie stills. A lot of kissing.

But none of it looked like anything real.

And yes, "real" was what I had just said I wanted. But now, fake and glam was looking a lot better than anything that was ever going to actually happen to me.

Fuck it. This whole therapy project was making me more depressed and confused than ever. I shoved the unfinished treasure map in my closet, called out for pizza and put *Notting Hill* in the DVD player.

●

Sunday around eleven-thirty, I was kneeling on the carpeted floor of Granola Brothers putting shoes back in their boxes when a pair of feet in gray rag socks and very, very old Birks stopped right in front of me. I looked up. Dark jeans. Belt with beads on it. Ancient plaid shirt. Flat stomach. Corduroy coat. Shell necklace. Hair shaggy enough to almost be considered long. Lovely thick eyebrows. Gideon Van Deusen.

"Ruby Oliver," he said. "Is that you?"

I stood up. "Gideon."

"What are you doing here?"

"I'm selling Birks," I said. Most Tate Prep students don't have jobs. They don't need the money.

"What a coincidence. I *need* some Birks!" he said.

I laughed and looked at his feet again. "Yours are old, yeah," I said. "Do you want the same kind again?"

"Wait," said Gideon, sitting down on an upholstered bench and crossing his long legs. He was at least six foot three. "I want to hear what you've been up to. Nora never tells me details. Are you still painting?"

Painting. He remembered.

"I have Art History this term. But I was using my watercolors just last night," I said.

Fletcher came over. "Is this a friend of yours?" he asked me.

Gideon answered, "Yes." Even though I was Nora's friend, not his. "But I came in for Birks," he added.

"Since your friend is here, Ruby, why don't you guys go have some chai?" Fletcher suggested. "It's quiet now. You can take a break for twenty minutes."

Fletcher was sending me out for chai with Gideon Van Deusen.

"I've got time," said Gideon. "But actually, I could use some dumplings. Do you want to get dumplings?"

Now I was getting a *meal* with Gideon Van Deusen. For a second, I forgot to feel neurotic and sorry for myself.

I was a girl to eat dumplings with, a girl with a job, a girl going for a meal with a boy she'd crushed on since sixth grade. I felt lucky and pretty.

Gideon and I walked through the Market to the Chinese snack stand. We each got a paper dish of vegetarian dumplings and doused them in soy sauce, rice vinegar and hot oil, then strolled to a bench and sat down. I could hardly look at Gideon's face, I was so nervous.

Not because I liked him, exactly.

But because he was older.

And because the way his dark eyebrows framed his chocolate eyes made him seem thoughtful.

And because not very long ago I was a silly middle-schooler who wrote "Ruby loves GVD" on her sneaker.

"How's the zoo job?" Gideon asked, his mouth full of dumpling.

He remembered I had a zoo job! "I got fired for defending the rights of a pygmy goat," I told him, and explained about Robespierre and the drunk dad. "So now I am reduced to selling Birkenstocks."

"Why reduced?"

"No offense, but they're not my idea of an acceptable fashion statement." I stuck out my feet and wiggled them.

Gideon stuck his feet out too. "Homely, but you can't deny the comfort," he said.

I shrugged. "My toes get cold." Here we were, talking about feet. Had a day and a half working at Granola Brothers brainwashed me so much that I considered feet an interesting topic for conversation? I changed the subject. "What are you studying?"

Gideon told me how he was taking guitar lessons and writing an essay on carvings by the Native Americans of the northwest coast. When he talked, he moved his hands a lot, and looked me in the eye, as if he really wanted to share his ideas.

I half listened while I stared at him. Gideon had lived outside the Tate Universe for a year and a half. He no longer concerned himself with bake sales and parents' nights and the flower deliveries on Valentine's Day. He didn't think about where to sit in the refectory or read old gossip about himself on the bathroom walls. He was nearly an adult. We finished our dumplings and he walked me back to Granola Brothers. I sold him a new pair of the same exact sandals he owned, without him even trying them on. "I'm so glad I ran into you," he said, smiling. Making his thoughtful eyes light up.

●

The next weekend, I went to Nora's place and helped make the magic chocolate chip cookies she'd told us about. The ones that had made Gideon clean her room and loan her his iPod. But first we made miniature molten chocolate cakes in ramekins. Nora taught me how to beat egg whites until stiff and then fold chocolate into them. I kept yelling, "It's an emulsion, people!" even though I wasn't sure it really was an emulsion, technically.

We were dumping the chips into the cookie batter when Gideon walked in.

"What are you doing here?" Nora asked him.

"I brought my laundry home."

"You kidding me."

"No. It's cheaper, even figuring in the cost of gas. Plus my sister is making cookies!" He came over and stuck a finger into the batter. "Hi, Ruby. How's the job?"

"Good," I told him. "A little smelly sometimes."

"Feet," said Gideon.

"Exactly."

While Nora and I baked, Gideon trotted from his car

to the basement several times. I couldn't help looking at his bare arms as he lugged his basket through the kitchen.

Later, he folded his stuff on the kitchen table. He was a good laundry folder. All the corners of his shirts lined up. And I thought:

1. Gideon hasn't gone out with anyone I'm friends with or used to be friends with.
2. No one I know is secretly in love with him and saying she's going ask him out.
3. He didn't make out with Ariel Olivieri and then refuse to speak to her.
4. He wouldn't leave me a note and then say it was nothing important.
5. He knows how to fold laundry and has attractive arm muscles.
6. Gideon Van Deusen has the sort of qualities I should look for in a boyfriend. He is straightforward and normal. He is outside the Tate Universe.

Nora, Gideon and I ate a few of the magic cookies and watched *Moulin Rouge* on DVD. When I handed Gideon a cookie, I silently wished his leg would touch mine during the movie.

And it did.

I didn't second-guess myself, and I didn't wonder if I really had feelings for him or was just using him as a substitute because I was lonely. I didn't think about Noel and I didn't think about Jackson and I didn't have a panic attack. I just sat there and got us all to make a list of movies besides *Moulin Rouge* where the heroine is a prostitute with a heart of gold[2]–feeling Gideon's warm thigh against mine.

●

Very early Monday morning, Meghan and I met Nora at school and set up the CHuBS recruiting table. As people drifted into the main building, Meghan and I tried (as we had on several previous days) to get people to sign up by bribing them with snacks—in this case, the miniature molten cakes and magic cookies. Nora left us with the baked goods and went to the darkroom to do yearbook stuff, printing pictures of sports teams and club members.

"I need to try the magic cookies right now," said Meghan. "Who can I try them on?" She scanned the hall-way. None of the candidates for Operation Sophomore Love was anywhere in evidence.

"I'm not saying they definitely worked," I told her. "I'm saying my leg was touching Gideon's."

"For how much of the movie?"

"Um . . . seventy-two percent."

Meghan squealed. "That's a lot! That's deliberate leg-touching. Was it a long movie?"

I nodded.

"Okay, so how did it work?"

---

[2] Here's the list we came up with, with help from the Internet. Movies that make prostitution seem like a glam job in which you might end up falling in love with a supercute and quality guy such as young Christian Slater or Ewan McGregor: *Moulin Rouge; Pretty Woman; Trading Places; Milk Money; The Girl Next Door; Risky Business; Irma la Douce; From Here to Eternity; Klute; Memoirs of a Geisha; L.A. Confidential; Night Shift; True Romance.*

"I gave him a cookie, and while he was eating it, I thought about what I wanted him to do."

Meghan crinkled her nose. "But it *was* Gideon."

"So?"

"So, he's the one who did Nora's bidding before. Maybe the magic cookies only work on him. Maybe they won't do anything to other boys."

"Which is why you have to try them on someone else," I said.

"There's no one to try them on."

We sat there for a minute. A few geeky freshmen wandered by. Varsha from swim team came and signed up to make pecan-caramel squares. She took a chocolate cake on a paper plate.

"Maybe," said Meghan, "we can eat the cookies ourselves and make a wish for something we want to have happen."

I doubted it would work, but I didn't want to squash her idea. All I'd had for breakfast was carrot juice and an apple. "Let's try it," I said.

Meghan took a magic cookie for herself and one for me. "We each make a wish for something we want. Not world peace, just like the stuff Nora wished for—someone will loan you his car, someone will bring you a present, someone will kiss you today. Okay?"

"Okay."

I looked seriously at my cookie. I knew it was stupid, but it was also kind of like the treasure map I was supposed to be finishing, wasn't it? Like envisioning what you want in the world, putting your energy toward imagining things the way you'd like them to be.

"Do we wish while we chew?" I asked. "Or before we chew?"

"You're the expert," said Meghan. "You wished while Gideon was chewing, right?"

"Right. So decide on your wish, but don't wish until you're chewing. You ready?"

We bit into our chocolate chip cookies, brown-sugary and delicious, and I wished, fervently, that somehow, today, I would know what to do with myself when it came to boys. The treasure map. Jackson, Finn, Noel, Gideon.

I wished that something, anything, would happen to help me sort out how I felt.

I wished for a sign. An answer to my questions.

I closed my eyes while I chewed, and when I opened them—Jackson Clarke was standing in front of me. "Hey there, Ms. Roo," he said.

I choked and coughed.

"I can wait." Jackson slid into the chair next to me and looked at the Baby CHuBS sign-up sheet. He chuckled. "Finn Murphy is making brownies?"

I managed to swallow my cookie and answer him. "We have a campaign."

"What is it?"

"Tate Boys Bake."

"Baking is the new basketball," said Meghan.

"Ha ha."

"Seriously," I said.

"I do cross-country and crew, anyway," said Jackson. "I don't subscribe to the cult of basketball."

"The new crew, then," I told him. "The new thing that's cool for guys to do."

"Roo."

"What?"

"If it involves an apron, guys are not gonna think it's cool."

"There's no reason girls should be the only ones who contribute. The male population of Tate Prep needs to let go of their antiquated notions of masculinity."

Jackson shrugged. "If I give up my antiquated notions of masculinity, can I have a cookie?" He reached over to the plate.

"Hold it!" I grabbed his wrist. "You not only have to give up your antiquated notions of masculinity, you have to actually bake for the sale. Are you signing up?"

Jackson pulled his arm away, laughing, took a cookie and scarfed it before I could even think what I'd command him to do as he ate. "Those are amazing!" he said. "Did you make them?"

"Nora did," I answered. "But I was sous-chef."

"I didn't think you made them.[3]"

"I creamed the butter and sugar," I said. "I pressed the button on the mixer and kept it pressed until Nora told me to stop."

---

[3] Ag. What did that *mean*? This is the kind of statement that makes it exceedingly difficult to talk to your ex-boyfriend.

Jackson reached for another cookie "Hey!" Meghan complained. "Are you signing up or not?"

"I'm not signing up," he said, biting in. "But I have a proposition for you." He took off his jacket and unwound his scarf.

"Make yourself comfortable, why don't you," I said.

"Remember I stopped by the other day and you weren't here?"

Yes, I thought. You left me that frogless note.

"I couldn't tell you what it was about with Wallace standing right there, but I'm running the Parents' Day Handicap and I need a covert base of operations."

The Parents' Day Handicap is not a tradition at Tate Prep—not yet. A senior boy who was a friend of Jackson's started it only last year. On Parents' Day, all the upper-school parents stroll through Tate looking at science projects, art exhibitions, yearbook layouts and videos of sports victories. Then they cluster into the auditorium and hear speeches from the heads of various departments—science, music, drama, English, etc.—talking about the wilderness programs, the school plays, the new electives on offer. Each department head is only supposed to talk for four minutes, because while the wealthy parent body is well inclined to pony up donations after a day of being assaulted with the wonders of the Tate Prep education, they also get bored if any of it goes on too long.

However, these are teachers. They are used to filling an hour-and-fifteen-minute class period with musings on the subject of light and dark imagery in *Hamlet*, causes of the French revolution or emulsions. They tend to ramble on. And Parents' Day is not like the Academy Awards. No music comes on to tell the long-winded it's time to shut up.

So the senior—his name was Sky Whipple, but everyone called him the Whipper—he had this idea to make odds on how long the teachers would talk. You could place a bet, a real money bet, on a particular department head. Depending on general tendencies to blather, the activities of the department and placement in the evening's program, the Whipper gave you odds. A long-winded teacher, early in the night, whose department had undergone radical changes? He'd be the favorite, paying out maybe two dollars for a dollar bet. A shy teacher speaking last might earn you fifteen bucks on the dollar as a long shot.

Jackson explained that he was taking bets and wanted a central yet unobtrusive location where people could find him before school. Could he hang for a couple of mornings at the Baby CHuBS recruiting table? Then, on Parents' Day night, after the speeches, he could sit at the bake sale table and pay out to the winning bettors as if he were innocently making change.

"What's in it for us?" asked Meghan.

Jackson shrugged. "If you're trying to get guys to sign up, maybe me sitting here would help? You've got a very girly operation, otherwise."

That was true. "You'd add manliness to the bake sale," Meghan said.

Jackson laughed. "Exactly."

My heart was pounding, like it always did when Jackson was around.

Was he flirting with me?

Was he talking to me to get back at Kim for something?

Was he trying to be friends?

"If you're going to sit here, you have to talk to everyone who comes by about how cool Baby CHuBS is going to be and how we're going to raise all this money for Happy Paws," Meghan was saying. "You have to encourage people to sign up."

"I could do that."

"Guys. Get the guys to sign up," she clarified.

"Can I get a commission?" Jackson asked.

"What do you mean?"

"Like, for every guy I rope in, you give me a free cookie?"

"No way," Meghan said. "It's us doing *you* a favor. And after what you did to Roo last year, you should count yourself lucky we're willing to help you out at all."

Jackson blushed. "Point taken," he said. Then he nudged me with his elbow. "I'm older and wiser now," he told me. "So can I sit at your table?"

My face was hot. I nodded.

"Okay, we have a deal. I can give you a tip: Ms. Harada is a long shot with a good chance this year. Wants support for her art and wilderness program." Jackson popped the last of his second magic cookie into his mouth.

As he chewed I looked at him hard. If I was over him, why couldn't I concentrate whenever he was around?

Why did it hurt so much when he flirted with me?

Or when he flirted with Meghan?

Why did I feel guilty for just talking to him, as if I was betraying Kim, who didn't even like me anymore?

He was chewing, and digging in his backpack to find his pen, and I wished on the magic cookie.

I wished for everything to be easy between us.

To feel relaxed around him.

For all the leftover pain to disappear.

Bad move.

12.

I Embark on a Doughnut Enterprise

Roo,

It's been more than a week since Crystal Mountain, and still, *Noboyfriend*.

Should I ask him out? Maybe to go watch the boys' lacrosse game?

Circle one: Yes or No.

You will notice I am writing you a middle school–type question-naire note. I guess I'm desperate.

Say you'll still be my friend despite this failing.

Nora

—crumpled in a small ball and passed to me during Am Lit while Wallace was trying (and failing) to make his laptop show us a PowerPoint slide show.

R: *Of course I am still your friend.*

N: *You didn't circle Yes or No!*

R: *This is 21st century. Hello? So Yes.*

N: *But I asked him skiing already.*

R: *Not the same thing. That was a group event.*

N: *You're right. I'm going to ask him. I have liked him for way too long to wait anymore.*

R: *Yay.*

N: *What if he says no?*

R: *Don't angst. He will say yes. You are gorgeous. And he already loves your cinnamon buns.*

N: *Cinnamon buns not enough.*

R: *Plus you like to watch sports on TV. You are every guy's dream.*

N: *What if he's busy? Then I won't know whether he wanted to say yes or no.*

R: *At least you will have asked.*

N: *Gideon was flirting with you the other night.*

R: *A little, maybe. He is out of my league.*

N: *Not.*

R: *Yah. It was just a mercy flirt.*

N: *If you get together with Gideon, and I get Noel, we can all hang out together.*

R: *I'll just hold my breath for that one.*

N: *We'd be like sisters!*

R: *You know I only date pod-robots.*

Of course, most of what I wrote was a lie. Well, not precisely a lie, because I do think girls should ask boys out and I do think Nora is gorgeous and any guy would be lucky to have her, but what I wanted to write was "Can't you just move on and like somebody else instead of fixating on Noel, especially when you are a nicer person than I am with better hair and way bigger boobs? Because even though I ate dumplings with Gideon, and even though I wished his leg to press against mine, if Noel starts liking you back, I might die of sorrow."

But I didn't write any of that. I wrote what I wrote.

Because I loved Nora.

And I wanted to her to be happy.

And I *had* been flirting with Gideon, and it was so nice of her to want me to go out with her brother. It was ridiculous and wrong for me to act like I had the slightest claim on Noel.

But was it so bad to want Nora to be happy with someone *else*? Some nice basketball muffin, or a student government type?

And why was it that I had to lie to my friend in order to do the right thing by her? In order to be a good person, I had to pretend I didn't feel the way I felt.

Was that what good people did? Denied their feelings and acted fake?

Nora didn't ask Noel out that day anyway. Or the day after that. She kept saying "Today is the day," but the boys' lacrosse game came and went without her asking him. So much for the Imitate Nora Van Deusen Program for a Happier Mocha Latte.

"If you ask Noel to Spring Fling, I'll ask a sophomore," Meghan said to Nora at lunch Friday.

"Spring Fling again?" I said. "Meghan, it's not even Valentine's Day."

"Which sophomore?" Nora asked.

"I don't know," said Meghan. "Which do you think?"

"If you don't know, it doesn't matter to you like it matters to me," said Nora. "It's not a fair trade."

Meghan laughed and ate her taco.

Nora didn't ask Noel out.

●

Thursday night was my night to cook for the Baby CHuBS recruiting table. And yes, I decided to make doughnuts. Call me pathetic, I won't deny it. Jackson had implied he doubted my baking abilities, and now I was going to make doughnuts. Just to show him I could.

I got a recipe off the Internet, rode my bike to the corner store for ingredients and started mixing dough. I expected Mom to throw a fit about deep-frying activities in her raw-food kitchen, but she just said, "I have to go over to Juana's for a bit now."

In case you forgot, Juana is my mom's best friend—the playwright with thirteen dogs and four ex-husbands.

"Why?" I asked, trying to figure out which thing in the drawer was a ladle.

"I have to pick something up." Mom put on her coat.

"What?"

"It's private," Mom said, smiling like she was someone special.

Whatever. I was making doughnuts. I wasn't going to get dragged into the Elaine Oliver show right then.

She left. Dad was working at his desk, composing a newsletter about early spring plantings.

I got out flour, baking soda, eggs, milk, butter, sugar and all that. I created an emulsion of butter and sugar creamed together that would have made Fleischman proud. My batter turned into dough as I added flour. I rolled it into a nice little ball, and . . .

Damn. Now I was supposed to chill the dough for two hours. How could I have not read that part of the recipe?

I stuck it in the freezer for half an hour.

Now to heat oil in the big pot we used for pasta (back when my mother let us eat pasta). The recipe said 365 degrees.

How was I supposed to tell when it was 365 degrees?

I looked at the bottom of the recipe. "Special equipment needed: candy thermometer."

I had no candy thermometer.

Who has a candy thermometer? That's like a highly specialized item.

I called Meghan first, because she lives near me, but she didn't have one, so I called Nora.

Nora didn't pick up the phone.

Gideon did.

"I thought you were at Evergreen," I told him.

"I don't have classes on Fridays, so I drove home this afternoon," he said. "Nora's at a yearbook meeting."

"Do you guys have a candy thermometer?"

"Uh, maybe."

"Could you check? Because I have a Doughnut Enterprise that requires a candy thermometer."

"Would I know one if I saw one?" The sound of Gideon rummaging through a kitchen drawer.

"Maybe. Wouldn't it look like a thermometer?"

He laughed. "You don't know what it's supposed to look like?"

I opened the freezer to poke the dough. "No. I decided to make doughnuts for our bake sale recruiting table and I'm like halfway through and I realized I need a candy thermometer."

"I think this is it. Hold on," Gideon said. "Mom! Is this thing a candy thermometer and can Ruby borrow it?"

I couldn't hear what she was saying, but Gideon eventually said: "She doesn't want to loan it out."

"Tell her it's a doughnut emergency," I said.

"She's having a doughnut emergency," he said.

"Oh, and tell her it's for charity," I said.

"It's for charity," he said.

"And tell her it will look good on Nora's college applications if CHuBS does well."

Gideon laughed. "She already said yes. Should I drive it over?"

Oh.

Gideon was going to drive a candy thermometer over to my house. Was it possible the other night hadn't been a mercy flirt at all?

So sue me. I changed my shirt and put on red lipstick before he got there. Most any girl would have done the same.

Gideon made a lot of noise about the houseboat. How cool it was, how he drove past the rows of Seattle houseboats all the time and had never been inside any of them, how much he liked the greenhouse, how amazing it must be to have so much nature right in your home.

My dad ate it up, of course, and raised his eyebrows at me in a hopeful way, as if to say, "Is this polite, intelligent and bohemian young man a new boyfriend? Can I begin to hope that you will become well-adjusted?"

I felt sorry for Dad for a second—because I know he worries about me—but then he pulled a complete Kevin Oliver move by saying, "Gideon, it's so nice to see Ruby has a new friend. I know she was lonely over winter break when Meghan and Nora were away."

I felt like retching. "He's Nora's brother, Dad."

"Okay. But he can still be your friend."

I was sure Gideon was going to run away screaming any second, but he walked over to the stove and asked me what I was measuring with the candy thermometer.

"Oil," I told him. "To fry the doughnuts."

"Can I watch?"

"Oh, um. Sure."

We put on oven mitts and measured the temperature of the oil until it was 365 degrees. In between testing the oil, I rolled out the dough and cut circles in it with a cookie cutter.

Gideon stayed. He helped me put the circles into the oil with a spatula.

They fried and turned brown! It was amazing.

We scooped them out with tongs and shook powdered sugar over them. Gideon ate one before it was cool and burned his mouth and had to suck on an ice cube. I got a splatter of oil on a vintage sweater that probably wouldn't come out, plus a small burn on my wrist. Still, we had doughnuts!

And more doughnuts.

And more doughnuts.

We spread them on cookie trays covered in paper towels to soak up the oil. When the table was full, we put them on plates on the dining room chairs and on top of the credenza behind the sofa. We didn't talk that much—just "Watch out, that one's getting too dark" and "Here, your turn with the spatula," stuff like that.

We had taken the last batch of fried deliciousness out of the oil when my mother came back from Juana's.

With a Great Dane.

My stomach dropped.

"Surprise, Ruby!" she yelled, standing in the doorway and letting the cold air rush in.

Oh my God. She had believed me about the dog.

How could she have believed me?

The dog was beautiful, but *enormous*. His head was as high as my chest and he had pointy ears and a tail like a whip. He was spotted like a Dalmatian and barking in a friendly way.

Rouw! Rouw!

My mother had a leash on him, but as he lunged into the house, she bent down and unclipped it. "Welcome to your new home, big boy. Say hello to Ruby."

The dog ran over to me and smelled my hand, then licked me from fingertips to wrist in one giant swipe of tongue. "Hiya, puppy," I said.

I love the way dogs want to lick you right away if they like you. They're so direct.

He sniffed Gideon briefly, then ran to the table. In a matter of seconds, the dog stood on his hind legs with his forefeet on a chair and ate an estimated twenty-two doughnuts. He spilled several trays and dusted the floor, the rug and one edge of the sofa with powdered sugar.

Oh no. All our hard work. All our deliciousness.

"Polka-dot, no!" My mother dashed over and grabbed him by the collar.

Polka-dot turned and gave her an enormous lick across the face, then ate another doughnut.

"Stop him!" I cried, and Mom was still saying "no"—but Polka-dot outweighed her by probably forty pounds, and he was very much enamored of the fried deliciousness that was my Doughnut Enterprise. Mom yanked him, and Gideon went over and yanked him, and frankly, Polka-dot was too strong for both of them. He was willing to come off the table, but then he just began scarfing up the doughnuts at chair level. I felt like crying, but my mom and Gideon had lost control, so I went over to Polka-dot and tapped his nose, like I'd seen Juana do when her dogs misbehaved. "No!" I said firmly.

Polka-dot licked me and ate another.

I tapped his nose again. "That's people food!" I said.

He looked at me as if to say, "Isn't it good stuff? Thank you for sharing!"

I had to admit, it would have been funny under other circumstances. He just looked so sure that I was going to understand his point of view. Still, a tear leaked out as I moved the single undamaged tray of doughnuts to the top of the refrigerator. I had worked so hard on them. Jackson would have been so impressed.

We just let Polka-dot have his way after that. He ate everything that was left on the floor. The four of us stood in silence, watching as he poked his head under the table, his tail snapping back and forth in doggy joy.

"At least he's cleaning the floor," said my father, who had been no help whatsoever during this entire escapade. "There won't be a speck of powdered sugar left when he's done."

Polka-dot wagged his tail.

"So I got you a dog, Ruby," said my mother, stating the obvious. "Like your therapist said you should have."

"Mom!" I'm not ashamed that I go to a shrink, but it's still not a factoid you want broadcast to hot college boys who are helping you cook. I mean, Gideon is so well-adjusted that the idea of mental illness must completely repel him.

"I knew Juana had a Great Dane," Mom explained. "So I went and got him for you."

"I wasn't serious!" I cried.

"You weren't?"

"No! It was a joke."

"Tell me that's not true."

"Therapists don't tell you what dog breed to get. Why would you think I was serious?"

"I don't know," said my mother. "Maybe because that's what you told me when we were having a serious conversation about your therapy?"

Gideon grabbed his jacket. "I should be getting home," he said. "It's late. Sorry about your doughnuts, Ruby."

"Oh, that's okay!" I said, as brightly as I could, while my face flushed with shame. Not only did he know I went to a shrink, now he also knew that I lied to my parents and fought with them.

So much for any attraction he might have felt. "Why don't you take a few home for your family?" I said, to cover my embarrassment. "I don't have enough to bring in for the bake sale recruiting, anyhow."

"Okay," he said. "They'll love 'em." As I wrapped four doughnuts for him, Gideon held out his hand to my dad. "Thanks for having me over, Mr. Oliver."

My dad shook enthusiastically. "Call me Kevin."

"And Mrs. Oliver, nice to meet you."

"I don't know what you were thinking, Ruby," my mother snapped at me, ignoring Gideon completely. I handed him the doughnuts. He gave me a quick wave and walked out the door.

My mom and I had a full-on argument over the mess in the house, my lie about the dog, her behavior toward Gideon, my lack of gratitude for Polka-dot and who knows what else. I cleaned the kitchen, wrapped the last two doughnuts in foil for my dad and Hutch to eat the next afternoon and spent the night sleeping on the couch so that Polka-dot—whose enormous people-food meal had seriously disagreed with him—could be taken out for walks every hour when he whimpered at the door.

●

I didn't bring my stupid treasure map to Doctor Z; I pretended I needed more time. We spent most of our Tuesday session talking about Polka-dot and how my parents had been transferring all their obsessive worry about me onto him: Polka-dot wasn't getting walked enough. Or he was walking too much and didn't he look like he might be limping? Or he was lonely at night and should sleep with them; no, he needed privacy at night and was content on the living room couch.

He shouldn't be allowed on the couch.

No, he was one of the family now, of course he could get on the couch! Endless discussion.

"It sounds like they love him," said Doctor Z.

I thought about it. "Yeah, they do," I said. "They've *fallen* in love with him, even though they didn't want him at first."

"Why did they get him if they didn't want him?" she asked. I hadn't told her about my lie.

"They got him for me," I told her.

Doctor Z crossed her legs. "That's a big present."

"I guess."

"Getting you a Great Dane when they didn't want one themselves."

My mom had been so pissy with me about Polka-dot—saying stuff like "You asked for him, you walk him"—that I hadn't had a minute to think about it that way.

She had gotten me a big present.

One she didn't want around.

As a surprise.

Because she thought it would help my mental health.

Because she loved me.

13.

I Am Wearing the Wrong Bra

Roo,

Here, in late payment for services rendered, four apricot Fruit Roll-Ups.

Also, in compensation for unforeseen hardships associated with the job of bodyguard,

one candy ring in a flavor that appears to be blue raspberry,

though I am not certain.

In any case, it is blue.

And I am blue.

Roo, I don't know what I did, exactly,

because I am a fool,

because I am not good with girls,

because sometimes I'm all wrong when I'm around you.

You know that, right?

Yes.

Everything has been all wrong between us since the bodyguard thing. I confess I don't know exactly what I did, but

I did something wrong.

And for the something, I am sorry.

Noel

—found in my mail cubby Wednesday morning, written on yellow legal paper and folded in quarters, taped onto a brown paper bag containing four apricot Fruit Roll-Ups and a blue candy ring.

Noel and I hadn't spoken more than we had to since the argument about Crystal Mountain. We had done our labs in Chem tersely and without amusement. I didn't sit by him in Art History. I was mad about Ariel, and Nora, and about Noel not understanding why I might be mad, and I felt spazzed out in general around him, so I just acted as cold and silent as I could. That way, at least, I wouldn't end up saying anything more I'd regret.

But I got his note Wednesday morning and I couldn't stay mad. There's something about seeing a guy's feelings written down, something about him taking that risk and committing his heart to paper, that means so much more than anything he could just say.

I read the note over several times and tasted the candy ring.

It was gross, actually, but no one had ever given me a ring of any kind before.

And here was one from Noel.

An apology ring. A sweet ring. A blue ring.

I tried it on and would have worn it for the rest of the day, but I knew I'd have to explain to Nora where it came from, so instead of wearing it, I wrote Noel back on a blue Post-it and stuck it in his mail cubby.

> *Sometimes, actually, you are very good with girls.*
> —R

I wasn't going to feel guilty about writing back, I told myself. It was the only polite thing to do. I couldn't go saying nothing when Noel had given me candy and Fruit Roll-Ups, could I?

And anyway, what I wrote was short. It wasn't like we were having some epic correspondence Nora didn't know about.

Yeah, my note was a little flirty. But Meghan flirted with everyone all the time, and it didn't mean anything. It was simply an expression of her personality. Flirting is a normal part of human interaction. Just because I flirted with Finn when we got him to join Baby CHuBS didn't mean I liked him back. It was only a way to pass the time. And just because Jackson had been sitting at our bake sale table making witty remarks—that didn't mean anything either.

So there. It was fine to write Noel back. I was going

to Chemistry and I was normal. It was nice to be friends.

When I walked into class, Noel's grin was so wide and open I knew he'd read what I wrote. Everything was easy between us again.

That day's experiment was a ginger ale volcano. We were supposed to put on these beige plastic smocks, which were exceptionally unflattering, and Fleischman gave each pair of lab partners a screw-top bottle of ginger ale, Altoids and small pieces of paper.

"My vanity is challenged," I said to Noel. "I hate it when we have to wear smocks."

"I have no vanity," he said, "but I'm sweating in this thing."

"That's it," I said. "We're not wearing them." I shrugged mine off, took Noel's from him and hung them back up.

"People!" called Fleischman. "I'm not going to make it mandatory, but I think you want to wear your smocks."

"Captain of the Beaker," said Noel. "Prepare the experiment."

"Smockless," I said, "I will do your bidding."

I rolled a stack of Altoids into a small tube of paper, quickly opened the pop and dumped the mints into the ginger ale.

Boom! The ginger ale exploded out the top of the bottle and sprayed all over the room. Ours was first.

Boom! Boom! Boom! The others followed.

Fleischman was ecstatic. Everyone was laughing and

wiping their faces, and some boys were trying to drink the pop as it foamed out the top of their bottles.

Me, I was wearing a white T-shirt. With a bright orange bra underneath. And no smock.

I was soaked in ginger ale.

"Nice rack, Oliver," said Neanderthal Darcy from the table on the other side of us.

"Heh heh heh," chuckled obnoxious Josh, his eyes glued to my boobs. "This is the best Chem class all year."

I looked at Noel. He was drenched too, but he was wearing a navy blue hoodie over a black T-shirt. And his eyes were going exactly where Josh's and Darcy's were.

My anchor coat was in my locker three stories down, and I knew if I ran out of the room I'd end up making the whole debacle more dramatic than it already was. I looked at Ariel and Katarina, hoping one of them would have a sweater handy and take pity on me. They were both wearing their smocks, so I couldn't see their outfits, but neither one was taking any action.

Fleischman was oblivious. He was talking to a table of kids whose ginger ale hadn't exploded properly.

Should I run out of the room and get my coat?

Or walk over to the closet and put a smock on?

Should I brazen it out and let everybody see my bra?

Don't panic.

Don't panic.

"You could stop traffic with those, Oliver," said Darcy. "The color's bright enough."

"She could stop traffic without the bra too," chuckled Josh.

"Excuse me," I said. "I'm wondering: Did your mothers raise all of their children to be sexists, or were you two singled out specially?"

"Don't get offended," Darcy said. "Orange is a good color on you!"

Josh nudged him. "Check it out. She's cold."

I crossed my arms over my chest.

"How could you tell?" Darcy asked.

Josh cupped his hands in front of his chest, then wiggled his pointer fingers. "You can tell."

I couldn't think of anything snappy to say, so I turned to leave the room for my coat when I saw—Noel. Holding out his damp hoodie to me. Keeping his eyes steadily on the floor so they wouldn't rest on my boobs anymore.

I took it silently, flushed with gratitude and embarrassment, put it on and zipped it up. It smelled like green apple hair gel and laundry soap.

We finished the lab in silence, wiping ginger ale from the stools and floor, then writing up our observations and listening to Fleischman talk about bubbles and surfaces and I don't know what.

I kept thinking, I'm wearing his hoodie. I'm wearing his hoodie.

No guy, not even Jackson, had ever given me his clothes to wear. And even though it was wet, it was incredibly warm.

●

Right after class, I was in a bathroom stall wringing the ginger ale out of my bra and T-shirt when Kim and Cricket came in together.

"Just act like she doesn't exist," Cricket was saying. "Like Jackson doesn't exist. Neither of them are worth your time to even think about."

Were they talking about me?

They were talking about me.

"I can't believe he's hanging around her like that, sitting at her bake sale table, after everything that happened," Kim answered.

"She's always wanted him back, you know that," said Cricket. "Erase the whole thing from your mind. Those people do not exist."

Kim sighed. "That's harder than you think."

My stomach twisted. I wanted to bust out of the toilet stall and explain that I wasn't doing anything with Jackson and he was just doing the Parents' Day Handicap at our table, and couldn't we keep the truce we'd settled into before Kim and Jackson broke up? Because really, truly, I meant no harm.

Only, I stayed where I was.

Besides the fact that if I came out they'd know I'd been hiding with my feet tucked up on the toilet seat, listening to their conversation, nothing I wanted to say was entirely true. I *had* been flirting with Jackson. I did have moments of wanting him back, now that he was single and talking to me.

What kind of person was I?

Pretty awful, I had to admit.

I mean, if I was Kim, I would hate me. And if I was Cricket I would hate me.

How did I become someone I myself would hate?

"Come to my house after school," Cricket told Kim. "We'll rent movies and eat cheesy popcorn. I'll get Katarina, Heidi and Ariel to come too."

"Nothing romantic," said Kim. "I can't watch romantic movies in my current state of mind."

"Of course not."

"And no anime or I'll think about Jackson."

"Would I ever intentionally watch anime?" Cricket asked.

"No," Kim admitted.

"Action," promised Cricket. "Action where guys take their shirts off. That'll make you feel better."

Kim laughed. "Not *Troy* again."[1]

Maybe it was the mention of *Troy*. Cricket had convinced us to rent that movie so many times in ninth grade. It made me sad to think of them watching it again (because of course they would, despite what Kim said)—eating the popcorn Cricket always used to make with Cheddar, Parmesan and pepper.

Without me.

Thinking about it, I panicked. There in the toilet stall, my breathing grew short, my heart pounded, I could feel beads of sweat forming on my forehead. You don't need another description. Same horror show, same channel. I stayed in the toilet stall through my whole lunch period, holding on to Noel's hoodie for comfort.

I kept thinking: I can't go on hanging out with Jackson at the bake sale table.

[1] *Troy:* Basically, lots of war and shirtless men.

I can't go on liking Gideon a little and liking Noel a lot.

I can't keep pretending to help Nora get Noel while secretly wanting him myself.

●

After school, still wearing the hoodie, I convinced Nora to drive me to Dick's Drive-in so I could make up for the calories missed at lunch. We got milk shakes and three orders of French fries with tartar sauce and mustard and leaned against the hood of her car to eat, even though it was chilly out.

"Noel saved me," I said, having explained the debacle with the ginger ale and the orange bra.

"Just goes to show," said Nora, her mouth full of French fry.

"What?"

"Skin color is the best color for underwear. It never shows through your clothes."

"That's not my point," I told her.

"Bright orange bra is just asking for disaster," Nora went on.

"Really," I told her. "I have a point, and I want you to hear it."

She looked surprised. "Okay."

"My point is—" I didn't know the best way to say it. I took a slurp of my milk shake to buy time. "Noel rescued me like it meant something. Like he *wanted* it to mean something."

"Oh." Nora's face fell.

"And maybe I wanted it to mean something too," I said.

Our fries were gone, so Nora crumpled up our greasy squares of paper and threw them in the garbage.

"What do you want me to say to that?" she asked as she came back.

"I don't know."

She twirled a strand of her hair on her finger and sighed. "You know I've liked him for a long time."

"Yeah, I know."

"You told me you were just friends."

"We *are* just friends," I said, not wanting to lie but wanting to say what she wanted to hear. "I'm just trying to be honest with you."

Nora was silent for a moment. "Let me be honest back, then," she said. "You don't know how it is to like someone for a long time. To keep thinking he might like you back, and thinking he might like you back, and never being sure. Every day you think something might happen. Every day you tell yourself, probably not–but *maybe*. And then every day it doesn't. It's hard."

I nodded.

"So–it's just not fair for you to suddenly decide you like Noel just because he loaned you his hoodie, when I've been liking him for months," said Nora. She looked at me plaintively, then opened the car door and slid into the driver's seat. I got in next to her.

"There's more," she said.

"What?"

"Like, with you and Meghan. It's hard being friends with you sometimes."

My pulse quickened. I had been trying to be so good—encouraging, reliable, honest—and now she was saying I was hard to be with?

"I love you both, but you know."

"No, I don't."

"Guys are always looking at you and wanting you," said Nora. "You're so sexy all the time, with lipstick and stuff, and Meghan—well, she's just Meghan. The two of you sit there at the bake sale table flirting with everyone. I just can't be like that. I'm not that type."

"You think I'm sexy?" I blurted.

Sometimes I felt sexy, and sometimes I felt like a troll.

In any case, I didn't walk around all day *trying* to be sexy.

"Hello? Orange bra? Fishnets?"

I nodded. When she put it that way, she had a point. I was shocked, though, that she thought of me and Meghan as the same kind of girl. Meghan was experienced and enterprising and often annoying on the boy front.

Was I the same way?

It *was* true, I guess, that I was getting attention from Gideon, Finn, Noel and maybe even Jackson, while Nora was getting attention from—no one. And that despite all the horrors that resulted, I *had* had a real boyfriend last year, while Nora had been *Noboyfriend* for life.

And I liked wearing fishnets. And I did like the way guys looked at my legs when I wore them.

"So I guess I'm saying, please don't steal him," Nora went on as we pulled out of the drive-in parking lot.

"I'm not trying to steal him," I said. "I'm just trying to talk about it."

Nora kept looking straight ahead. "It's not fair for you to have Gideon and Jackson and half the soccer team flirting with you, and then decide you're interested in the one guy I like when you could have almost anyone. Don't you see what I'm saying, Roo?"

I had never thought of myself that way. As flirting with half the soccer team. But with CHuBS recruiting, I couldn't deny it was true.

I looked at Nora. Her hands in fuzzy blue gloves. Her skin tan from skiing. Her lips a little chapped. Her eyes on the road because she's always a good driver, even when she's upset.

I didn't want to be the slut most people at school thought I was. I didn't want to be the boy-stealing flirt Nora obviously thought I might be. I wanted to be a good friend. The kind of friend who gets invited over for *Troy* and cheesy popcorn when something bad has happened.

"Point taken," I told her.

●

"Ruby, did you make the treasure map we talked about?" Doctor Z asked next Tuesday, when I told her about the drama.

"No. But I'll get to it, I promise."

Doctor Z looked at me.

"I've been superbusy," I said. "Did I tell you about the SAT practice tests? They're making us do practice tests. I spent my Saturday night doing that."

She looked at me some more.

"Plus all the Baby CHuBS stuff, plus I have to read *House of Mirth*. Plus"—I spit it out—"I had another panic attack this morning. Just randomly before I left for school."

She crossed her legs and still didn't say anything.

"Are you mad I had the panic attack? Because you're right, I should be over them by now."

Doctor Z shook her head. "I'm not mad. This is not about me being mad or judging you in any way, Ruby."

"Sorry."

"You don't need to apologize," said Doctor Z. "I'm wondering if we should spend some time examining your resistance to making the treasure map."

"I don't know what I want!" I yelled. "How can I make a map of what I want when I don't know what I want?"

Silence from Doctor Z.

"I want Jackson one day. I want Noel another day. I want Gideon another. Sometimes I want random people I don't even like especially, like Finn Murphy or my Am Lit teacher."

"Um-hm."

"I want something real one day and I want something like in the movies the next. I'm not consistent, so I don't know how on earth I'm supposed to do this assignment."

"I see."

I sat there for a minute or two. "What should I do?"

"I can't tell you that," said Doctor Z.

"Then we're not going to get anywhere," I told her, "because I don't know what to do myself. I know you always say I should take action to get what I want out of a situation, but if my mental health is so bad I don't even know what I want, there's no action to take."

"Lots of people don't know what they want."

"Yeah, but are they mentally stable?"

"Possibly."

I stared at her.

Doctor Z chewed her Nicorette. After a while, she said, "I can offer you an observation, for what it's worth."

"What?"

"The treasure map assignment was to create a map of positive peer-group relationships—a friendship collage."

"Uh-huh."

"The map you've been describing, based on what you said just now about Gideon, Jackson and Noel, is more like a treasure map of *boys* rather than friends."

Oh.

"When we're talking about these people, we're talking about love relationships, are we not?"

"Um. Maybe not love, exactly."

"Romantic relationships."

"Yes."

"I think that's an interesting interpretation on your part."

"What do you mean?"

"I mean that you interpreted peer-group relationships as romantic relationships."

Oh yeah. That.

"That's why I'm here," I told her. "My priorities are completely warped."

14.

I Suffer from Rabbit Fever

Dear F-SHAN (Former Secret Hooter Agent Noel),

The hooters of F-SHAR (Former Secret Hooter Agent Ruby) are sincerely indebted to you for their heroic rescue last week. Despite the closure of the Hooter Rescue Squad, your skills remain sharp and your instincts unwaveringly chivalrous.

F-SHAR has kept your hoodie much longer than she meant to, but now it's clean and she can give it back. In the interim, she begs you to accept this package of Band-Aids that look like bacon strips, as a sign of her sincere appreciation for your efforts.

—written on white typing paper in black pen—after several drafts; folded in thirds and wrapped around a package of bacon Band-Aids. Shoved with hoodie into Noel's mail cubby.

i hadn't thanked Noel properly for the rescue, since after my conversation with Nora I felt self-conscious every time I talked to him. But finally I did the laundry and I had to give him his hoodie back, so I wrote this note trying to be amusing and unromantic.

At the start of junior year, before Nora liked him, before he asked if he could kiss me, back when we were friends without any added weirdness, Noel and I had formed a top-secret agency devoted to protecting the rights and interests of hooters everywhere. It was subsequently disbanded. Long story. Anyway, the note was a flashback to the days of the Hooter Rescue Squad, when we were friends, just friends. I stuck it in Noel's cubby on Thursday morning.

I bought the bacon Band-Aids at Archie McPhee. It's this amazing store on Market Street that has things like windup nuns, Devil Duckies, pirate garbage cans, action figures of Sigmund Freud and Jane Austen—and the world's largest collection of snow globes. I got Noel the bacon Band-Aids, even though I'm a vegetarian, because it was so perfect that the bacon was the right shape. Also because Mr. Fleischman had sent home a Chem handout on hydrogenation and how bacon fat is solid at room temperature and liquid when heated and how you could make soap from it too. The Xerox included a photograph of bacon—as if Chem students couldn't be relied upon to have a clear idea of what bacon was without visual assistance. Noel and I had laughed about that a lot when we first got the handout: "What's bacon, again?" he kept asking. "I can never seem to remember. I hope it's not on the test."

Thursday lunch, Noel wrapped three of his fingers in

bacon strips. He waved them at me across the refectory, and I got my raisin salad and went to sit with him, Nora, Meghan and Hutch.

Hutch was wearing fingerless gloves and his usual biker jacket with "Iron Maiden" painted on the back. He didn't talk much, not around Meghan and Nora, at least. I wasn't sure if it was because Hutch didn't like *them*, or because he worried they didn't like him, but he was definitely different at school than when he worked with my dad in the greenhouse.

While we ate, Meghan, Nora and I put on the serious pressure for the boys to contribute to Baby CHuBS.

Hutch shook his head. "You don't want to eat my cooking, trust me."

"Noel?" Nora pressed, leaning across the table and tapping his arm. "Won't you help us out? It's for a good cause. Ooh, excellent Band-Aids." She touched his hand. "What happened to your fingers?"

Noel smiled at her. "I didn't burn myself baking, I'll tell you that."

"Does it hurt?" Nora pushed out her bottom lip sympathetically.

"Nah," said Noel. "I'll live."

"So bake for us!" she said.

"I'm not much of a cook."

"But your parents cook," I said. "Your parents are cooking fiends. You could use some of your mom's recipe books. Does she make French stuff, like pastry?"

Nora turned to me. "When were you at Noel's house?" she asked.

"In the fall," I said. "When you couldn't go to *Singin' in the Rain* with us."

"Oh," said Nora, in a voice that had that slight edge to it—that edge that meant, I didn't know you'd been to his house.

Hutch laughed. "Ruby dragged you to *Singin' in the Rain*?" he teased Noel. "Dude, you have no willpower."

Noel put his head on the table in mock shame. "Apparently I cannot say no when Ruby makes me do girly stuff. First a musical comedy, now baking."

"Ruby's not making you," said Nora. "I am *asking* you, very sweetly."

Hutch slapped Noel on the back. "You know what you need?"

"What?" Noel said, turning his face toward his bottle of orange juice.

"You need to go see Van Halen at KeyArena."

"Oh no," I said. "He does *not* need that. You do not need that, Noel."

"You think that will counteract my sissy baking?" Noel asked Hutch, lifting his head.

"That was an official yes!" cried Nora. "You heard it here, first, guys."

"David Lee Roth is a rock legend,"[1] said Hutch, still talking about Van Halen.

---

[1] *David Lee Roth:* Fronts retro-metal band Van Halen. The man has been known to wear studded chaps *without pants underneath* and to pair that article of clothing with a gold breastplate and an off-the-shoulder shirt. I think that's all you need to know.

Noel put his head back down. "If I make French pastry, I don't know if even Led Zeppelin would be strong enough to counteract it."

"Will you really do French pastry?" I asked. "What does your mom know how to make? Can you make pain au chocolat?"

Noel groaned.

"It's not sissy baking," said Meghan. "Several guys on the soccer team are already signed up."

"She's right," said Nora. "It's manly manly baking."

Noel lifted his head. "She can make pain au chocolat," he said, with faux resignation. "I'll get her to show me how."

"Yay!" Nora clapped her hands.

Noel stood to bus his tray. "Ruby, I am powerless to deny you, but you may be the death of me."

Hutch laughed. "You can come over and play Guitar Hero this weekend if you need to reclaim your manhood."

"I may need to," said Noel.

When the boys left, Nora's forehead wrinkled. "He's powerless to deny you?" she said to me.

I held up my hands in innocence.

●

At my next week's therapy appointment I told Doctor Z about the conversation with Nora, the Hooter Rescue Squad note I wrote to Noel and how I'd gotten him to make pain au chocolat for the bake sale.

Doctor Z listened quietly and then she said: "Explain to me again how your note read?"

"The one I gave Noel?"

"Yes."

"It said thank you for . . . um . . . rescuing my boobs. Only I called them hooters because that's the official term used by the Rescue Squad."

"Hm."

"What?"

"You wrote the note after the conversation with Nora, am I understanding correctly?"

"Yes."

"But you don't feel you were flirting with Noel."

"No."

"Some people might say that writing a note about your breasts to a boy is a flirtatious thing to do."

Ag.

Ag, ag, ag.

I had written a note about my breasts to Noel.

What kind of girl writes a note about her breasts to the boy her best friend likes?

What kind of girl writes a note about her breasts, period? Was I in total denial, flirting with Noel when I'd promised not to? Was I a horrible person?

How had I let myself do that, after my promise to Nora?

There has got to be a word for the general but inadvertent sex mania I've been having. I mean, this is probably how rabbits feel, and why they're always procreating at unreasonable speed. Like they don't even mean to be thinking about sex, much less doing anything sexy, and then they suddenly find themselves in the throes of horizontal action, or whatever position rabbits do it in. They find themselves doing it and having a whole rabbit family without even meaning to, just like I find myself looking at Wallace's chest hair or flirting with Jackson or pressing my thigh against Gideon's or *writing notes to Noel about my boobs*.

Ag again. I am completely Rabbity. I have Rabbit Fever. That's what's wrong with me.

That and panic attacks. And being a roly-poly, of course. And being a rotten friend.

"Ruby?" Doctor Z was leaning forward.

"Yes?"

"Try to be here, now, okay? You have my attention."

This is something Doctor Z has taken to saying often. "Be here, now." Like when I start thinking of all kinds of stuff that I'm not telling her and tune out that I'm even in therapy and that someone's even there waiting for me to talk. Be here, now.

"Okay," I told her. "I'm here." And I burst into tears.

15.

I Should Resist, but I Do Not Resist

Dear F-SHAN,

I am sorry I wrote you that note about my hooters. Completely inappropriate.

Suspect I am possessed by strange demon.

Am researching quality exorcists.

Please, please, forget it ever happened.

—written on a half-sheet of notebook paper and folded in quarters.

the day after my therapy appointment, I put the note in Noel's mail cubby. After Chem, he grabbed my arm and pulled me down the hall and up the stairs. "I want to show you something," he said, but when we got to the painting studio on the top floor, it was empty. The room had a sky-light and cool winter sun shone into the room, which was filled with easels and half-assed student paintings. It smelled like turpentine.

"What?" I said. "I didn't think you were taking painting this term."

"I'm not," said Noel. Then he put his hands on my shoulders and said, "Really, I want to *tell* you something, and I knew we could be alone here."

"You're not showing me anything?"

"No." He laughed nervously.

"What do you want to tell me?"

"Well." I took his hands off me and walked around the room.

"What?"

"Anything I say is going to come out stupid."

"You brought me here," I told him. "You might as well say it."

"Okay." He kept pacing back and forth. "I—I'm dying to hear about your hooters."

"Excuse me?"

Noel wiped his hand across his forehead. "That came out wrong."

"You think?"

"I mean, you don't have to say sorry about that note you wrote me."

"Thanks," I told him. "But I talked to my shrink about it and she pointed out that if I don't want people to think

I'm a famous slut, I shouldn't, you know, do slutty-type stuff."

"It wasn't slutty," said Noel, standing still, finally.

"Yeah," I said. "It pretty much was."

He took a step toward me. "It wasn't slutty. It was sexy."

Oh.

He thought I was sexy.

"I want to hear *everything* about you, all the time," Noel said. "Hooters—or whatever."

"You do?"

"I really do," he said.

I felt so dizzy-happy that he told me this, though I knew I shouldn't even be there with him, though I knew Nora would be mad, though I knew there were so many things wrong about all of it.

Because I wanted to hear everything about him all the time too.

It all rushed over me, the happiness and the guilt and the confusion. I put my hand out to steady myself on the counter, and as I did, Noel leaned into me and put his lips on mine.

He didn't ask if he could kiss me, the way he had last time.

He just did it, so I couldn't say no.

His mouth was so soft, much softer than anyone else I'd ever kissed, and as I put my arm up to touch his neck he seemed frail, underweight, vulnerable. And yet also, a little bossy. I mean, he had just decided to kiss me, when he knew I'd said no for good reasons before, but he was not taking no for an answer this time.

I pulled away, in what I fully admit was a lame attempt to protest, and Noel pushed his whole body against mine as I leaned back against the art table.

Then there was nothing to do but kiss him some more.

He wrapped his arms around me like he was hugging me, not trying to cop a feel or whatever, and I just surrendered to the dizziness and kissed him, with all the tension draining out of me. Forty weeks of *Noboyfriend* and all my anger about Ariel and all my guilt about Nora and confusion about Jackson and Gideon, all my Rabbit Fever and everything—just washed out.

I was happy.

Noel pulled back. "That's what I wanted to say, actually," he breathed.

"I didn't quite hear you," I told him. "I think you need to say it again."

So he did, and we were kissing and the world was spinning—and then the door to the art studio opened and Ariel Olivieri was staring at us.

Ariel.

My dizziness left me abruptly and the art room seemed sordid.

I had been kissing Noel.

Whom I had resolved not to kiss.

Whom I had promised not to kiss.

Whom Ariel had kissed.

Ag.

Ariel would be furious, of course.

Then she'd tell Kim and Cricket.

Kim and Cricket would tell Nora.

I would lose all my friends.

I deserved to lose all my friends.

He was off-limits; I had said so myself.

Ariel turned and slammed the door behind her, and I hate myself even more for what I did next: I took off my glasses and kissed Noel again. And again, and again. It was like the Rabbit Fever took over and I couldn't help it. I felt bad while I was doing it, but I also felt fantastic. I had been wanting to kiss him for so long, and he wanted to kiss me, and the room spun again and the sordidness disappeared and it was just him and me, together. I jumped up to sit on the table and wrapped my legs around him and blocked out everything else but the feel of his body against mine.

It was even better than retro metal.

●

I spent the rest of the day experiencing delicious jolts of happiness alternating with long periods of self-loathing.

Noel was crazy about me! And I was crazy about Noel.

I was a bad friend.

My love life was sorted out, I had left the state of *Noboyfriend,* he would call me tonight like he said he would and we'd go to the movies and there would be more kissing and everything would be wonderful.

No. That couldn't happen. I was a crazy leg-wrapping slut who kept on making out with a guy even when I'd told my closest friend I wouldn't steal him.

Noel was crazy about me!

I was afraid of running into Nora, even though we had

no afternoon classes together, so I hid out in the library. But then I had a panic attack.

Full-on. Couldn't breathe.

I went into the bathroom and was kneeling on the tile floor, trying to slow my heart. I found myself wishing with all my soul that Doctor Z would give me a diagnosis of panic disorder so I could get some pills that would straighten me out. Life would be so much easier, so much better, if I could just pop a little green pill each morning that would make me act like a normal person. Normal, like I'd have consideration for the feelings of others, sound judgment and healthy friendships. Normal, like I wouldn't be so selfish and slutty. Then maybe I could also have a purple pill to calm me down when I felt panicky, something that would short-circuit my brain? That way I wouldn't have to sit on the floor of the bathroom holding a damp paper towel and crying because I couldn't breathe.

Maybe I could talk Doctor Z into a prescription. Medication would make all of this go away.

Then I got scared of myself for wishing such a thing. Not that medication is bad if you need it, but wishing for it to solve all your problems? That's the attitude that makes people start drinking at two in the afternoon and then they wind up a sick alcoholic like my uncle Hanson.

I leaned against the cold door of one of the bathroom stalls and tried to get my breathing under control, but tears were running down my face. I wanted Noel. I had always wanted Noel.

Now I wasn't going to get to have him.

Or if I did get to have him, I'd lose Nora and Meghan.

I was a backstabbing slut and I wanted pills and I'd lost my zoo job and Ariel was going to make everyone hate me and why couldn't I disappear out of the Tate Universe and never see any of these people ever again?

Couldn't I move to Australia and commune with koala bears?

No, I had SATs in a month. And I had History of Europe starting now. There was going to be a quiz on Friday.

I ran the cold water and splashed my face. Blew my nose repeatedly and got myself into some kind of shape to reenter society. Though to be honest, my nose and lips were still completely swollen from the crying, I had no eye make-up on anymore, and I was not at my most attractive.

I left the bathroom and headed to the library doors, my eyes on the floor.

"Whoa, Roo, what's wrong?" someone said.

Jackson, heading in with a book tucked under his arm. I was next to him before I even saw him.

"Nothing's wrong. I'm fine." We were standing in front of the circulation desk.

He squinted at me. "You look upset."

I shook my head.

Jackson reached out and touched my cheek with his spare hand. "Come on. I can tell you've been crying."

I shook my head again, and tears spilled silently across my cheeks.

"What happened?" Jackson set his book on the floor

and hugged me, his puffy parka soft and comforting, like a pillow.

It felt so familiar and so strange at the same time. I had a rush of déjà vu, because of course I'd hugged Jackson more than I'd hugged anyone else on the planet in the last six years.

"You don't have to tell me what's wrong," Jackson said. "But you're crying. I'm not going to let you tell me you're fine."

I turned my head because I was scared I would get snot on his jacket. It felt good that he cared.

I don't know how long we stood there, but eventually he pulled away from the hug, patted me on the back.

"I'm okay," I said. "Really."

"You sure?"

I nodded.

"You sure sure?"

"Yeah."

"Okay, then." Jackson bent to pick up his book. "Feel better."

Then he headed for the stacks and was gone.

I had wished on the magic cookie for all the badness between us to disappear, and now, maybe, it had.

●

When I got home that afternoon I took the cordless into my room and called Noel.

"I can't go to the movies tonight," I told him.

"Why not?" he asked.

"Noel, I'm so sorry, but I can't go anywhere with you.

Today was . . ." I didn't have the words. "Today was, it was . . . I think it was a mistake."

"Why?"

I started babbling on about the thousand reasons not to kiss him, and how I liked him but I couldn't betray my friend Nora and did he realize Nora liked him too? Because it was probably obvious, but I wasn't supposed to tell, and here I was betraying her again by telling but I wanted to be a good friend to her.

I was in no shape to be going out with anyone because I was unbalanced, and he knew I had the panic attacks and they weren't getting better, in fact they were getting worse, and I was really sorry, I should never have kissed him back and had he ever heard of Rabbit Fever?

"Ruby." Noel interrupted me.

"Huh?" I hadn't finished explaining.

"Look. I understand if you can't go out with me. But you could at least tell me the truth about it."

"What?"

"Tell me the real reason. I mean, haven't we been friends long enough that I deserve the truth?"

"I don't know what you're talking about."

"The problem is not the situation with Nora."

"Yes it is," I said. Because it was.

"Ariel saw us. You know she'll tell Katarina and all those guys, and it'll get back to Nora by the end of tomorrow. That's a done deal and nothing we do or don't do is going to change it. Nora is going to know."

It wasn't what I wanted to hear. "Maybe she won't tell," I said.

"This is Ariel we're talking about," Noel reminded me.

Okay. He was right on that. "But maybe Nora will forgive me if she knows it was just once. If she knows how sorry I am and how I never meant to hurt her."

Noel sighed. He and I both knew that probably wasn't true. She had told me outright not to steal him, and back in sophomore year, Nora had been furious at me when I'd kissed the wrong boy. She hadn't forgiven me for months that time. A second infraction would be even worse.

But I was *trying* to be a good person. It was completely against my nature—but I was trying. Couldn't Noel see? And even if Nora wasn't going to forgive me, at least Meghan might. More important, I had to be able to forgive myself—which I never would be able to do if I became a flat-out boyfriend stealer.

"You're not being straight with me," Noel said.

"What do you mean?"

"Be honest with me about why. That's all I'm asking."

"I'm trying to be honest!" I said. "I have bad mental health!"

"I saw you with Jackson this afternoon at the library," he said. "I was on the mezzanine."

Oh.

Oh no.

"You were making out by the circulation desk."

"No we weren't."

"I saw you," Noel said.

"We weren't making out."

"Okay, let's call it a clinch. Can we call it a clinch?" His voice was bitter.

"No, it was a hug."

"Look, if you're back with Jackson now, whatever, that's fine. I just want to know now, so I don't have to hear it through the Tate Universe rumor mill."

"I'm not back with him."

"It's obvious something was going on, Ruby, and it was only like two hours after you'd been with me. I have to say, I felt sick watching you."

Oh no oh no oh no.

Noel was the only guy in the whole school who didn't think I was a slut. The only one who said he knew for sure that I hadn't done all the things people said I'd done.

And now, I knew he was thinking maybe I *had* done those things. What is more slutty than making out with two different guys on campus in the same day?

"It was a hug," I repeated. "He was hugging me."

"I don't care about the technicalities," said Noel. "I just know there's no way I can compete with Jackson Clarke. Not in cross-country, not in popularity and obviously, not with you."

"Noel, I–"

"I just wish you'd been straight with me. When you called me tonight, I wish you'd said, 'Hey, Noel, I'm back with my ex-boyfriend. Sorry.' I wish you'd been truthful."

"I was!"

"Come on. You made up this excuse about Nora when obviously that situation is already going to be what it's going to be, and then you talked about your panic attacks, and both of those are just a front. Because what it's all about is Jackson Clarke."

"Noel, please."

"I'm hanging up now, Ruby," he said. And the phone went dead.

It did not escape my notice that he'd said the same thing to me as Doctor Z.

That it wasn't all about Nora. It was all about Jackson.

Was that really true?

16.

I Encounter Horrible Feet

Roo,

   I got all your messages on my cell. I got your e-mail and your note. But I don't know what to say. I've liked Noel for so long, and you were my closest friend. I know you have mental health issues, but I still don't see how you could do this.

   I really, really don't want to talk about it with you. Please, just leave it be.

   Nora

—e-mail, received by me, Thursday morning.

I had left Nora a note in her mail cubby Wednesday after my panic attack. I had called her four times and when I couldn't reach her, finally, I'd sent a long e-mail explaining that nothing more was happening with Noel and I was desperately sorry.

By way of answer, I got the e-mail above, Thursday before I left for school.

I told Meghan the whole thing while she was driving me to school. The Seattle rain was pouring, like it always does in winter, and we were inching through traffic.

"Wait, back up," said Meghan, slurping vanilla cappuccino. "You like Noel?"

I nodded.

"You've liked him all this time?"

I nodded again.

"Am I blind?" she said, pulling onto the freeway. "Because I had no idea. This is a major news flash on the Meghan end."

"I tried to tell Nora," I said. "But she just asked me to stop liking him. So I wasn't exactly advertising it."

"Oh, that's fair of her," said Meghan sarcastically.

"I was trying to be a good friend."

"You can't stop liking someone you like," Meghan reasoned. "Was he a good kisser?"

"That's what you want to know? I've ruined my life."

"Well, was he?"

"Yes, but I'm never kissing him again anyway, so it doesn't matter. Ariel will have told the whole school by now."

"I don't think Nora will stay mad," Meghan said

thoughtfully. "It's not like Noel was ever going to like her back."

"You think not?"

"Obviously not."

"You were always so encouraging to her about him."

"I didn't want to squash her hopes," Meghan said, "but I could tell by how he acted at Crystal Mountain that he knew she liked him and wasn't interested."

"Really?"

"Don't worry. Nora will realize the truth of the situation and be over the whole thing before lunch. Listen, if I were you, I would have done the exact same thing."

Yeah, but Meghan was a girl who hadn't had a single female friend until last year. And for good reason.

"Look at it this way," she went on. "Noel likes you, you like Noel. Neither of you can help it. It just happened. You can't angst so much about it, you have to follow your feelings."

"It *didn't* just happen," I said. "I flirted with him. I wrote him notes." I wrote him notes about my *boobs*. "I'm a bad person."

"You are not." Meghan squeezed my knee. "You just liked a guy and you could tell he liked you back, so you acted on it."

I shook my head. "I did to Nora exactly what Kim did to me last year," I said. "I stole the guy she liked." My cappuccino was going cold in my hand. I was too upset to drink it. "What kind of person would go out and do the exact same thing that ruined her whole life when someone did it to her?"

"Nuh-uh." Megan honked at a small blue sports car that had cut in front of her. "That is *not* what you did."

I hunched into my anchor coat. "It pretty much is."

"Roo, you and Jackson were *going out*. You had been going out for months."

"So?"

"Nora just liked Noel. She barely even talked to him on the phone or anything. If she thinks that's anything like the same as you and Jackson, she is seriously inexperienced."

But the thing was—Nora *was* seriously inexperienced.

"She's not going to be mad for long," said Meghan confidently. "We're all friends. Give her a couple days, and clear things up with Noel and everything will be fine. Maybe you should send him flowers for V-Day. I'm thinking of sending some to Mike. And maybe Don."

"Noel hates me," I said.

Meghan pulled into the Tate Prep parking lot. "No one hates you, Roo. Noel just got jealous. You worry way too much."

I was ridiculously glad that *Meghan* didn't hate me, even though I would never understand the way her mind worked in a million years. As soon as we got to school, I went to the Valentine's Day table in the refectory and ordered her two dozen carnations.

●

Nora ate lunch with Kim and Cricket. She didn't meet my eyes in Am Lit. She looked away whenever I passed her in the halls. But ninth period I cornered her in the darkroom.

She was bent over the enlarger, fiddling with the focus on a photograph of the men's heavy eight posing in their boat. The room glowed a soft red, and there was the sound of running water. There was no one else there.

"Nora?"

She unbent at the sound of my voice. "Roo, I asked you to just leave it."

"I need to apologize," I told her.

"You've apologized six different ways already. What else are you going to say in person?"

She had a point. "I thought maybe we could talk about it, figure things out between us."

Nora put her hands on her hips. "The only thing to talk about is how I don't want to talk about it."

"But—"

"You went behind my back, you took the guy I liked, you did everything the same as you did last year, and no amount of apologizing or saying you're not going to go out with him now—nothing is going to erase it."

"Nora, I'm sorry."

"You should have thought of that before you kissed him. You should have thought of that before you lied and said you wouldn't steal him."

"Can't you just try and understand?" I begged her. "It's not fair for you to just stop speaking to me without even listening to my side. I tried to tell you how I felt when we went to Dick's. I told you about the ginger ale and the hoodie."

"And then you said you wouldn't steal him."

"I didn't mean to lie about it. I was trying to be the person you wanted me to be."

"Roo. Please just go. I have to get these pictures done."

"Nora, we've been friends since sixth grade. Can't you cut me some slack? Do I have to be perfect all the time, or we're not friends?"

"Please go!" Nora yelled.

I stood there, trying to think if there was anything I could say that would make things better. "It just seems like friends should forgive each other," I said lamely. "Or at least try to understand each other. Not shut down completely."

"If you won't leave, then I will," Nora snarled at me.

She grabbed her bag and walked out of the darkroom, leaving her negatives on the table and the light on in the enlarger.

●

Over the next two days, my life was like a movie entitled *Return of the Roly-poly Slut*. Meghan and Hutch were the only people to even speak to me. Hutch gave no indication he had any clue what had happened, but he did do a stealth coffee run one afternoon when he was working for my dad and brought me a surprise cappuccino. So maybe he felt sorry for me.

I had two panic attacks.

Trying to get my mind off things, I called Granola Brothers and asked if they had any extra hours for me to work over the weekend.

"Sure, dudette," said Fletcher. "You can work till eight

on Saturday instead of four—and if you want to come in for Jo-Beth on Sunday at ten, she has a birthing class she wants to go to. You can sub for her until two."

So I went in. It was a good distraction. The only bad part of the job was the feet. When people came in to try on shoes, they had to be fitted barefoot. Birkenstocks have these special footbeds that mold to your feet as you wear them, and you have to make sure the customer's foot is fitting properly in there or else the shoes won't be comfortable. So for a good chunk of a working day I was on my knees buckling sandals onto sweaty winter feet. Feet with chipped toenail polish, feet with hair, feet with black gunk underneath the nails, feet with misshapen toes, all kinds of feet.

Fletcher and Jo-Beth and the other people who worked at Granola Brothers were seriously committed to the health of feet. They wanted everyone to leave the store with shoes that were going to change their whole attitude toward footwear. And I have to admit, my Birks—hand-me-downs from Meghan—were comfortable. So comfortable that I had started noticing the way my Mary Janes pinched around the toes, and the way my Vans didn't have a whole lot of arch support.

While I was working my late Saturday shift that weekend, a tall, long-haired guy about forty-five years old came in. The store was busy, and he stood there looking at a pair of suede Arizona-style and patting them the way people do when they're not quite sure they want to try something on. He was wearing a hand-knit sweater and jeans. He had white skin and hair that used to be red but was now graying. Deep grooves on either side of his mouth, like he smiled a lot, and little rimless glasses.

"That's our most popular style," I told him. "Would you like to try them on?"

He looked at me as if he was surprised I worked there, and said, "Yeah, that would be great."

He told me his shoe size and I went in the back and brought out a couple of pairs for him to try on for fit. He took off his boots and a pair of old, used-to-be white tube socks and happily revealed the strangest, hairiest, smelliest feet I'd ever seen. I mean, I had seen a lot of feet by this point, but these were especially horrible. I tried not to gag as I buckled him in. He must have had some kind of fungus on his toenails, or between his toes. Something was not right.

"My girlfriend thinks I should start wearing these," he said. "The air circulation is supposed to be good for the skin, yeah?"

I stood up to get away. "The air circulation is a benefit, but people also wear them with socks in the cold weather," I said, gesturing at the sock wall. "The footbed molds to your sole and gives you ideal arch support."

He paced the floor with a spring in his step. "These feel good. How do they look?"

Aside from the fact that I could see his disgusting feet, they looked fine. At least, as fine as Birkenstocks can *ever* look. "I think that's your size," I told him. "As long as they're comfortable."

"My girlfriend is meeting me here soon," he said. "She's across the way buying vegetables. Do you mind if I wear them around the store for a few more minutes until she arrives? I'd like to have her opinion."

"Knock yourself out," I told him. "And investigate our sock wall. If you're looking for air circulation, you're going to want only a hundred percent cotton."

"Hey, thanks!" He smiled and went over to the socks and started looking at them with impressive earnestness.

I headed for the door of the store and opened it for a moment to get some fresh air after the strange and funky smell of his feet. As I stood there, I saw a familiar sparkly orange poncho heading across the cobblestone street of the Market, past the Hmong tapestry place, along the aisle of batik blankets—

Doctor Z.

I had never seen her out in public before. I had never even seen her in the waiting room of her office or the halls of her building.

What are you supposed to say to your shrink when she's shopping?

How nice to see you, what a cute poncho?

Ooh, what did you buy?

How's your weekend going?

No! You can't ask her anything, because you're not supposed to ask about her personal life. She only asks *you* stuff. And you can't update her on your mental health either:

Oh, about my insanity, I can kind of turn it off and function while I'm at work, isn't that interesting?

Or, Hey, I was going to tell you on Tuesday, but since you're here, I made out with Noel, got caught by Ariel, then hugged Jackson and got caught by Noel. Nora hates me and my life is falling apart.

Ag.

Doctor Z hadn't spotted me yet, but she was heading toward the shop. I shut the door of Granola Brothers and dove as quickly as I could behind the counter.

The bell jingled as someone opened the door. "Schmoopie!" cried the man with the horrible feet. "What do you think?"

I froze.

There was the sound of kissing. Schmoopie and the man.

Then, Doctor Z's voice: "They look good on you. How do they feel?"

"Nice!" he said. "Strange, though. I'm not used to this much arch support."

"You'll grow to love them," said Doctor Z. "Everyone does."

More sounds of kissing.

Ag.

I was so spazzed out I hit my head on the edge of the counter, knocking down a display of tie-dyed socks and letting out an involuntary squeal.

"Are you okay?" The man with the horrible feet came around to the side of the counter so he could see me.

"Fine, fine." I stayed seated on the carpet, hidden from Doctor Z, collecting socks and sorting them into purple and orange. "Thanks for asking. Do you want to take those shoes?"

Maybe I could ring him up from down here, if he was

paying with a credit card. Maybe I'd never have to stand at all.

"I'm wondering if I should try them in suede," he said. "My girlfriend told me the suede is really comfy."

I had no choice. "I can get those for you," I said, and hauled myself to standing. "Hello, Doctor Z."

"Ruby." She smiled at me. "I had no idea you worked here."[1]

"Yes," I said, forcing my voice to be cheerful. "Well."

"Good to see you."

"Yes. Um."

The man with the horrible feet said, "Lorraine, do you know each other? What a wild coincidence!"

"Just from around town," said Doctor Z.[2]

"How great!" said her boyfriend. "Ruby, I'm Jonah." He held out his hand.

"Nice to meet you," I said, though I felt like passing out.

Did Jonah know all about me?

Did Doctor Z put her Birkenstocked feet up on the coffee table after a hard day and tell him all about her roly-poly client who couldn't keep any of her friends and blew off her therapy homework and kept having panic attacks and suffered from Rabbit Fever?

---

[1] Translation: "I see you every week for therapy and you never told me you got a new job. What do you think we're doing in those sessions your parents are paying for? Because you are obviously failing to tell me the most basic and everyday facts about your life."

[2] Translation: "She's a mental patient, but of course, since we're in public, I respect her confidentiality and won't reveal how I know her."

Ag and more ag.

It was so weird to see her out in the real world, holding a mesh bag full of winter squash and something wrapped in brown paper that was probably fish.

Honestly, I had never thought about Doctor Z *eating*. I mean, of course she ate. She had to eat. Everybody eats. But I never thought about *what* she ate, and now I knew what she was having for dinner, and that she was going to cook, and that she must really really like winter squash because there were several big gourdlike items in that bag of hers.

Who on earth likes winter squash that much? I mean, it's okay, but it's not exactly a pinnacle of deliciousness.

"Ruby helped me put the shoes on," said Jonah, pulling gently on his ponytail. "She thinks they're the right size."

"I'll get the suede for you to try. Be right back," I said, and ducked into the storeroom as quickly as I could.

I had also never thought of Doctor Z as having friends, much less *a lover*. And not just a lover in the abstract, but Jonah, an actual flesh-and-blood aging white hippie lover who called her Schmoopie and kissed her in the middle of shoe shopping. Which would actually have been cute and romantic—

1. If she hadn't been my shrink. Because it is almost more disturbing to think about your shrink having sex than to think about your parents having sex—which is already plenty disturbing, thank you very much. And—

2. If he hadn't had those horrible feet. Because not only was my shrink friendly with those horrible feet, my shrink actually lay down naked with her perfectly

normal feet (I had seen them in her Birks) next to his disgusting ones, which were no doubt smelling and fungus-ing up the bed every night, and—

Ag.

This whole train of thought was not good for my mental health.

Just treat them like customers, Roo, I said to myself. Pretend she's a colleague of Mom's or a friend's parent and put on your fake please-the-grown-ups smile and get it over with.

So that is what I did. Jonah liked the suede ones. He paid with cash. Doctor Z said, "Have a nice day, Ruby," and I nodded, but no words would come out of my mouth.

After they left, I sprayed the shoes he didn't buy with an antifungal mist we kept in the back for cases of possible contamination.

17.

I Choke on Ninja Deliciousness

Dear Oliver,

Since you've never run a CHuBS before, and your big day is coming up in a couple of weeks, I want to offer you some tips and reminders. I should have done this before—sorry! I've been so busy getting Spring Fling organized, and we're even starting to think about prom (!!) so I haven't had a minute.

Anyway, I wanted to remind you how many old-girl CHuBS will be at Parents' Day. For example, Spencer Hanson's mom, Mason Silvey's mom, etc. They have baked every year for the big December sale. You might remember Ms. Hanson's reindeer cookies? Yum! The legacy of CHuBS is important to these ladies, I just want you to know.

Also, it's great you've got boys contributing, and I'm excited about your deliciousness idea! But let's not forget that we know what sells, and we know how much the Tate community depends on the CHuBS tradition, and with Easter around the corner, we can take advantage of that. I heard you've been going through some ups and downs in your personal life, so give me a holler if I can bake anything extra or offer guidance about the sale.

—Gwen Archer

—written on a sheet of notebook paper in Gwen's round handwriting; folded in thirds and slid covertly across the table during French V.

translation: "I hear you're a big slut and everyone hates you, plus I'm worried you'll make an enormous debacle of Baby CHuBS because you're not doing it the way I would do it and I'm worried people will blame the failure on me. In fact, I'd like to fire you and run it myself at this point, but I don't have the guts, so I'm going to make you feel like crap and then pretend to offer help in the hopes that you'll step down."

I didn't reply to the note, and I ran away after French V so I wouldn't have to talk to Archer. I was too miserable to deal with her and her CHuBS agenda, so I avoided her in class and in the hallways and acted like I didn't see her waving me over in the refectory.

You might think *The Return of the Roly-poly Slut*—aka my life—would be an interesting movie. It might have nudity or some stylized violence, even if the acting was hokey. It might have wild costumes and play at midnight to a cult following.

But no. It was not an interesting movie. Just dull footage of a girl dressed in jeans and an old bowling shirt, reduced to a single friend.

Everyone at school knows Nora hates her now—though they may not know exactly why.

Everyone knows Ariel hates her too—and they *do* know exactly why. They know the girl made out with Noel in the art studio. And since everyone loves Ariel, they hate the Roly-poly Slut to keep Ariel company.

Heidi, usually polite enough in History of Europe, moves to the other side of the room to sit with tennis players, saying something smells like a rat. Katarina mutters "bitch" under her breath in the lunch line.

No one knows that Noel thinks the girl was in a clinch with Jackson, but they *do* know Jackson keeps sitting at the CHuBS table, and rumors are flying. The girl tries to speak to Kim one day after Am Lit, thinking maybe she can explain, but Kim says, "It's strangely quiet in here. Cricket, I don't think I heard anything. Did you hear something?" Cricket says "No, it's silent as a tomb." They walk away.

The girl changes Chem lab partners at the request of Noel.

She tries to avoid crying in Art History and Am Lit.

She helps people with hippie sandals.

She drinks carrot juice for breakfast. She does homework. And she walks a harlequin Great Dane through the Seattle drizzle.

●

Tate Prep has this Valentine's Day delivery service, run by the seniors. Everyone walks around all day with armfuls of flowers. Flowers in mail cubbies, flowers on desks, flowers delivered during class by cute senior boys. Lectures are constantly being interrupted by the entrance of someone or other with an armful of roses.

On February 14, a day on which I had no expectations of getting flowers from anyone but Meghan, I was sitting in Am Lit when Jackson walked into the room with a bouquet of twelve white carnations.

Everyone looked up when he walked in. Everyone meaning not just me but Kim, Cricket and Nora, too.

He caught my eye and headed over.

My stupid heart leaped, seeing Jackson with twelve white carnations, extending them to me.

I took them and read the card—"Hugs and Happiness! Nora"—and my eyes filled. Partly because no, of *course* they weren't from Jackson, and partly because I knew Nora wished she could take them back. Wished she'd never bought them. Just like the flowers I'd sent *her,* they'd been ordered when we were friends. Now they didn't mean anything at all.

"Thank you," I mouthed—but she turned her gaze away.

Even though Jackson was delivering flowers to people all across school—all the seniors were—Kim stared as he left the room with a look of shock and hurt in her eyes. I saw Nora whisper in her ear, probably explaining that those weren't from Jackson, they were the carnations *she* had sent me, though of course I hadn't deserved them after all.

My sessions with Doctor Z came to a standstill. I couldn't finish the treasure map. I couldn't talk to her. I couldn't listen to anything she asked me.

A typical session went like this:

Doctor Z: How are you feeling today?

Me: Okay.[1]

Doctor Z: Do you want to elaborate on that?

Me. Um. Not really.[2]

Doctor Z: All right. Well, I'm here and ready to listen.

Me: Okay.[3]

Doctor Z: (silence)

Me: I don't have much to say, that's all. I'm fine.[4]

Doctor Z: (silence)

Me: (silence)[5]

And that would be it.

So I wasn't getting anywhere in therapy, and the fact that I couldn't talk to my shrink was obviously taking its toll on my mental health. The panic attacks increased to

---

[1] Inside my brain: I can't believe your boyfriend calls you Schmoopie. Schmoopie Schmoopie Schmoopie Schmoopie!

[2] His feet are so disgusting. How can I tell my problems to someone who hangs around all day with a horrible foot smell?

[3] I mean, that was some really weird fungus Jonah had going on there. It's enough to make me doubt your judgment.

[4] Because if you feel like those are normal feet, Doctor Z, I can't possibly trust your evaluation of whether my brain is normal.

[5] I can't tell you anything I'm thinking because I know you'll be offended that I thought your boyfriend had freakishly repellent feet; it's not the kind of thing you can actually say to *anyone,* much less your shrink, whose personal life you're not supposed to know anything about.

the point where they made my life hell at least four times a week.

Only now, no Nora came to put her arm around me.

●

In early March, Spring Fling was announced at assembly. It was scheduled for April 6. Every year the dance takes place on a mini-yacht; there's a band and some punch and cake, and it's supposed to be a really romantic evening–much more so than prom, which is all about graduation and never has an amazing view or anything.

This year, I had no plans for going. I mean, what were the possibilities?

- Finn. Yes, he'd brought sample ninja brownies and lemon bars to us at the CHuBS table, and blushed, and convinced half the boys' soccer team to bake things, but it would have been social suicide for him to take me to a dance, given that he was Kim's ex.
- Jackson. We were on friendly terms; in fact, he had been sweet to me lately–but with all our bad history and the waves of hatred coming from Kim and her friends, no way.
- Gideon. Nora had no doubt told him I was evil. Besides, college boys never want to go to high school dances.
- Noel. Couldn't stand me.

Everyone else single was either Jackson's friend, Ariel's friend, a complete Neanderthal or unlikely to risk the horrible gossip that would circulate if they asked me to the dance—even if they imagined that by taking the school slut they'd probably get lucky.

The first mentally deranged thing about the whole situation was that I even *wanted* to go to Spring Fling. One formal dance I'd been to had been really awkward. The other had been a complete nightmare. There was no reason to think I'd actually have a good time, and if I'd been sane I just would've forgotten the whole dance was happening and gone about my roly-poly business. Except—

I heard Katarina, Ariel and Heidi in line for lunch, talking about dress shopping together over the weekend and how they thought wearing black was over and this year they wanted pastels. Heidi and Katarina were going with senior basketball muffins. Ariel didn't have a date yet, but she was thinking of asking Noel. "Or I bet I could get Sam Williams to ask me, don't you think?" she said, thereby illustrating the fundamental difference between me and her, as I was completely unable to conceive how on earth a girl would "get" a guy to ask her to a dance if he didn't want to take her already.

Kim was going with a guy she knew from crew team; Cricket had asked a senior she'd befriended in Drama Elective. Nora didn't have a date yet.

And neither did Noel. But then, last year he'd gone solo, so maybe he wouldn't ask anyone.

Anyway, I wanted to laugh with Meghan (who was no doubt going to end up going with some candidate for Operation Sophomore Love, though she hadn't decided which one yet). I wanted to worry about shoes and whether

I'd kiss my date. I wanted to order a boutonniere and buy a dress with my Birkenstock money. I wanted to try on makeup in department stores and slow dance at the end of the night.

The second mentally deranged thing about the situation was that I was waiting for someone to ask me. Obviously, this is the twenty-first century, and as I'd told Nora, girls can ask guys out. We *should* ask them out. There is no reason to sit around being passive and hoping that someone will ask you to a dance when you can easily invite the person you want to go with. How are women going to become president and win Oscars for directing if we sit on our butts waiting for things to happen?

I know this. I believe it. But I still wanted someone to ask *me* to the dance. Yes, like it was 1952. Yes, like Gloria Steinem never existed. Yes, idiotically, yes.

I don't know where all the dance fantasies came from. But there they were, these stupid retro dreams, and here I was, without them coming true.

A week and a half after Spring Fling was announced, Meghan met me by her Jeep in the parking lot holding a foil tray of brownies.

"Those look like ninja brownies," I said to her. "Are those ninja brownies? Because if they are, I need to have one now."

She didn't seem to be listening to me. "Roo, I have something I want to ask you."

"Actually," I said, "I don't care if those are ninja brownies. I'll take any brownie I can get, if the truth be known. My mother is making carrot-pecan burgers for dinner."

Meghan handed me the tray of brownies and got into the Jeep, unlocking my side. "Take whatever you want."

"But don't we need to save them for Parents' Day on Friday? Why is Finn giving them to us now, anyway? They're going to get stale."

Meghan started the Jeep and pulled out of the Tate parking lot. "They're not for Baby CHuBS, Roo. They're for me."

I choked on my mouthful of ninja deliciousness. "Finn made these for you?"

Meghan nodded. "That's what I wanted to ask you. Finn invited me to Spring Fling and I said yes. So I was wondering if you wanted me to see whether he has a soccer stud-muffin manly baking friend who could take you."

Oh.

All that blushing Finn did in the B&O Espresso.

And the baking.

And the recruiting of soccer players.

It wasn't for me.

It was for Meghan.

And I must be an egotistical wench, because even though I should have been happy for Meghan that she was going to the dance with a great muffin who obviously liked her if he made her ninja brownies, some part of me still thought, Wait, he's liked me since second grade! He's mine! You're not allowed to steal him even if I do think he's a muffin, and another part thought, It's so unfair that

Meghan has a real romantic date when she's been flitting around planning Operation Sophomore Love, and I have nothing and nobody and all I'm trying to do is be a good person.

However, I am at least sane enough that I didn't say any of that out loud. Instead I asked, "What about Dan and Dave and Don and Mike and Mark?"

Meghan shrugged. "They'll survive. They're way too young for me, anyway, even if they are tall. I mean, I don't think I can fall in love with someone who hasn't even taken the PSAT."

"It must be love if Finn is making you brownies."

That made her smile. "Nora and I went to the B&O two days ago to do homework, but she could only stay for an hour, and I stayed until six, which is when Finn got off work. Then he asked me if I wanted to go walk down Broadway with him and look in Marco Polo, you know, the travel store? So I did, but then I had to go into Rite Aid, so he came with me."

"And?"

"He asked me to Spring Fling and I said yes and then I kissed him in the middle of the drugstore!"

"You were still in the drugstore?"

"Yeah. I was just buying Noxzema. Not anything personal," Meghan said.

Ag. I would never wander the aisles of a drugstore with a potential boyfriend. It's like a minefield in there. Tampons! Zit medicine! Dandruff shampoo! Condoms! I don't know how we'd look each other in the eye after parading past all that stuff, much less start making out in an aisle full of diapers.

"That's great," I told Meghan.

"So do you want Finn to find you a date? I'm sure he would."

Suddenly, I didn't want to go to Spring Fling. Not with someone who was only escorting me as a favor to his buddy from the soccer team. Not with some bland muffin I didn't even want to talk to, much less slow dance with.

"Nah, that's okay," I said.

"You sure?"

"Yeah."

"You know you have to go dress shopping with me anyway."

"Of course I will."

"Thanks. Oh, and I have news of Noel," Meghan said, almost like it was an afterthought.

"What?" My heart jumped. Maybe he wasn't mad at me anymore. Maybe he was sorry he'd assumed I was a giant slut instead of believing what I told him about Jackson. Maybe he'd decided he loved me even if I *was* a giant slut. Or maybe, at the very least, he'd been asking about me.

"Nora asked him to Spring Fling," Meghan said, crinkling her nose. "And he said yes."

18.

I Fight the Tyranny of Cute

Parents' Day, Meghan and I got to the Baby CHuBS table by seven-thirty a.m., when the baked goods were scheduled to start arriving. Later on in the day, Archer and some other senior girls from CHuBS would take over sales; then Finn and some soccer muffins were doing the late-afternoon shift; then we closed for the teacher presentations in the auditorium. Meghan and I were returning for the hour after the presentations, when people would be milling around shaking hands in the main lobby. That was also when Jackson would be paying out to the people who'd bet on the winner of the Parents' Day Handicap.

We'd painted fresh Happy Paws signs, plus one that said DELICIOUSNESS! and one that said TATE BOYS BAKE. I had made little stickers to put on wrappers of things brought in by the guys: "100% Boy Baked."

The more breakfasty items were for early morning: ginger scones, chocolate chip muffins, oatmeal-raspberry bars, sour-cherry squares, cream cheese coffee cake. The serious dessert items we had scheduled for later delivery. Meghan was in her element, flirting with the soccer boys and any other male who was bringing in supplies, asking their advice on pricing, licking her lips provocatively whenever anything good came across the table.

Me, I was keeping track of how much attrition my roly-poly slut reputation had caused us. Nora, who hadn't shown up for anything Baby CHuBS–related since I'd gotten caught kissing Noel, did deliver her promised molten chocolate cakes and a tray of coconut-chocolate squares, because she's never been the sort to back out on a charitable commitment. Besides, she was still friends with Meghan. Varsha Lakshman and the girls I knew from swim team brought their stuff, as did Finn and the soccer muffins. But Ariel, Heidi, Kim and Katarina—all of whom had signed up to bring things because it was Nora's project—not one of them delivered what they'd promised. Neither did several girls who knew Nora from basketball. Neither did Ariel's crew-team cronies.

And neither did Noel. He was supposed to bring his pain au chocolat first thing in the morning, but he never showed up.

Not really a surprise.

Still, I did feel proud looking at the long table all spread with deliciousness, knowing I had been a big part of making it happen and that we'd raise a lot of money for Happy Paws. Parents started trickling into the main hallway about ten minutes before first period would normally begin. More moms than dads. Dads in suits or khakis and cheerful sweaters; side-parted hair; checking cell phones. Moms with blond streaks or well-cut bobs, expensive jewelry and deceptively casual jeans. The lawyers, doctors and stay-at-home parents of Seattle.

My mother arrived, dragging my dad by the hand, wearing a black cotton dress over black leggings with her hair frizzing out in wild curls. She was holding a tote bag that read: "If it's not a Great Dane, it's just a dog."

My dad, with gardening dirt still under his nails, wore a T-shirt that said simply: "The DogFather," with a logo like the movie poster for *The Godfather*.

"*That* is what you wear to Parents' Day?" I asked him, pointing at the shirt.

"We mail-ordered the both of them," my mother said, indicating her bag. "They came this morning after Meghan picked you up."

"Oh, Ruby, of course I'm *your* father too." My dad put his hand on my shoulder and gazed sincerely into my eyes. "I'll always be your daddy."

"My father *too*? You mean to say that you think of yourself as Polka-dot's *dad* now?"

Kevin Oliver looked at me with complete noncomprehension of the insanity of his statement. "He's a member of our family group, Ruby. You know that."

Mom said, "You shouldn't be jealous because we're celebrating Polka-dot. Polka-dot needs to be celebrated.

Goodness knows, he never got any personal attention while he was living at Juana's with twelve other dogs."

"Do you think he understands that you're celebrating him with T-shirts and tote bags?" I asked them. "How can he even tell?"

"Oh, he can tell," Dad said. "He came over and sniffed the tote as soon as it came out of the package. He was looking at the picture and saying 'Rock on, that looks like my brother!' "

"He did not say 'Rock on,' " I told them, putting a sticker on one of Finn's prewrapped lemon squares.

"He barked when Dad put on the T-shirt," added Mom. "And you know he never barks. He was telling us how much he liked it."

"Fine."

"Ooh, what have we here?" It was Mr. Fleischman, waddling up to the counter.

"Emulsions!" I yelled, because I knew it would make him happy. "Lemon emulsion, sour-cherry emulsion, cream-cheese-frosting emulsion. Take your pick. They're all made with science!"

He chuckled and rubbed his hands together.

"Mr. Fleischman," I went on, "these are my parents, Kevin and Elaine Oliver."

They all shook hands and Mr. Fleischman bought a sour-cherry square and a slice of carrot cake with three layers of cream cheese frosting. "Do you want anything from the bake sale?" I asked my parents.

My dad looked to my mom as if for permission. She gave a slight nod and he said, "Yes, I'll take a coffee cake."

"Two dollars. Mom, you want anything?"

"Nothing for me, thanks," she said, patting her tote. "I have a dehydrated banana–barley cookie in here if I get hungry before lunch."

Then, hand in hand, they wandered off in the direction of the art studio, where there was a display of student work.

"They seem like delightful people," Mr. Fleischman said. "I always get along with dog lovers."

Meghan sighed. "Your parents still hold hands. That's adorable."

"I'll sell 'em to either one of you for a dollar fifty," I said.

Meghan and I worked the bake sale table from eight to eleven and sold a ton. Finn's lemon squares were seriously, seriously delicious, though he put me off my feed by French-kissing Meghan behind the Baby CHuBS table. The coffee cake sold out, and by ten-thirty we had nearly run out of other breakfasty stuff. We were expecting a new influx of more desserty things around eleven, and sure enough, on the dot Archer showed up to take her shift behind the counter.

Only, she was not holding a tray of deliciousness. She was holding a tray of marshmallow Easter bunnies and–I kid you not–Jesuses.

The Jesuses were built like snowmen, standing three mallows high and crucified on crosses made of sugar cookies with chocolate frosting. "I meant to bring these earlier," Archer said, displaying them proudly, "but I had trouble getting the crosses to stand up properly. I stabilized them with clear gumdrops. I don't think anyone will mind, do you? You can barely see them."

Meghan and I looked at the bunnies and Jesuses. Archer had clearly spent hours on them. The bunnies had floppy ears made from strawberry Fruit Roll-Ups, tiny licorice-drop eyes, and tails made of white dinner mints. The Jesuses had hair and beards of chocolate, and each was dressed in a loincloth made from green Fruit Roll-Up. Yes, a loincloth, even though they each only had a single marshmallow at the bottom instead of legs.

"I see you're sparse here," said Archer, surveying the table.

We were sparse, because of the people who didn't bring their stuff, but I threw back my shoulders and told her, "People have been buying everything, that's why. We have more coming in to put out for the after-lunch crowd. This is just the end of breakfast."

Gwen shook her head. "I'm worried these items you've got here are not going to move, Ruby. Frankly, I'm surprised you let people bring in"—she gestured at the sour-cherry squares—"blobs of red stuff on pastry when the evidence of previous sales, and in fact the entire tradition of CHuBS for years back, is that cute sells."

"I told you we were going for deliciousness," I said. "I told you we were doing Tate Boys Bake."

"Yeah," she answered, "but you didn't say you were abandoning cute. It's hardly CHuBS if you abandon cute like this!"

"The lemon bars are amazing," piped up Meghan. "Two people came back and bought seconds. And the coffee cake sold out within a half hour 'cause we had such good word of mouth."

Archer ignored her. "At least I have my bunnies and Saviors," she said. "We can price them high and maybe that'll save your bottom line."

I was furious. How dare she come in after all my weeks of hard work and disparage my bottom line without even looking in the cash box? How dare she hand this whole project over to me and then criticize the way I did it? She wasn't even listening! She hadn't even tasted anything!

She wasn't considering how we'd gotten all these boys to become involved in the sale, how we'd gotten the word out about Happy Paws; she wasn't considering anything we'd done except how *she* wouldn't have done it that way.

And now she wanted me to sell Jesus marshmallows.

"Gwen," I said. "I don't think we can sell what you brought."

Archer's eyes widened. "What? Of course we can. Three fifty each, I think."

"I know Easter is in a few weeks," I said, "and Tate is certainly Christian-centric enough to have a Christmas dance for the middle school, even though people here are Jewish and atheist and Muslim and Buddhist. But I'm not going to have Saviors and bunnies at *my* bake sale unless we're representing other religions too."

"No one's going to mind," said Archer.

"There are *parents* here," I said. "Non-Christian parents of non-Christian kids. I don't think we should get religious about our baked goods at a school function unless we show some diversity."

"Besides," added Meghan. "I'm not sure about marshmallow Saviors, anyway. No offense, Gwen, but the Jesuses are a little much."

"They are not!" cried Archer. "They're cute and inspirational!"

"I think they're borderline offensive." It was Jackson, sliding into his usual seat on the far right of the table and opening the ledger in which he kept his Handicap bets.

"Exactly," said Meghan. "Even the Christians aren't going to like them."

"Clarke, why are you always ragging on me?" Archer barked.

Jackson shrugged. "It's fun?" He went back to his notebook, but poked my leg under the table in sympathy.

"Fine, don't sell the Saviors. I'll bring them to my church group this weekend," said Archer. "They'll appreciate them."

"We're not selling the bunnies, either," I told her.

"Why not?"

"Because that's not what you signed up to bring." I flipped through my notebook. "You signed up for dulce de leche brownies and white chocolate cupcakes with raspberry filling."

"I changed my plans," she said. "I'm sure lots of people didn't deliver exactly what they signed up for."

"That's not the point," I told her. "The point is, you knew what deliciousness meant."

"So?"

"You made marshmallow bunnies not to save my bottom line but to try and prove to me that you knew better. You're not trying to help me, you're trying to take control of my sale and prove I don't know what I'm doing."

"Go, Ruby," Jackson muttered.

Just then, three of Archer's senior CHuBS compatriots showed with trays of cutesy cupcakes: green ones with shamrocks that said "Kiss Me, I'm Irish"; vanilla ones with yellow lollipop flowers; pink ones with ice cream cone hats and smiley faces.

"See?" I said. "Those were not on the sign-up sheet. You're trying to take over!"

"Look, Oliver," said Archer as her minions began moving my deliciousness to make room for cuteness. "I've been on CHuBS since I was a freshman, and the sale I ran in December was the most successful ever. I only let you do Baby CHuBS because you seemed like a team player and last year you had good ideas for cupcakes. We have a legacy to protect. I told you, there are lots of moms here today who were CHuBS twenty-five years ago. They're not going to be happy seeing the whole thing looking ordinary, with lemon bars and brownies. Here you are, going against tradition with your whole deliciousness boy-crazy thing, and meanwhile, rumors are going all around school about you—and now CHuBS is going downhill."

"Don't bring my reputation into this!" I yelled. "Whatever rumors are going around have nothing to do with the bake sale, nothing to do with how much money we're raising for charity, nothing to do with anything. I staffed the thing well enough, didn't I? People are buying the food, aren't they? And maybe those CHuBS moms will love it that boys are getting involved. Maybe they'll be thrilled to eat actual food rather than marshmallow art projects."

"I hardly think so," said Archer. "Cute is a tried-and-true approach, Oliver. It's what people like. It's what brings in the money. And it's what CHuBS is all about. I'm sorry I ever gave you this job."

"I'm sorry too," I told her. "But you did. And I worked really hard on it, and so did Meghan, and I'm not letting you and your friends waltz in here and take over."

Just then, Finn came back to the table with four soccer muffins, all bearing trays of amateur baked goods that at the very least aimed for deliciousness. "We have plenty of supplies, thanks," I told Archer. "You can take yourselves and your cuteness elsewhere."

"Fine." She grabbed her tray of marshmallows and turned on her heel, her friends in pursuit.

As I looked at her retreating back, all the fury of the past couple weeks surged inside me. Not just at Archer, but at everything. I picked up a piece of carrot cake and lobbed it at her retreating back. It hit her head, stuck in her hair and then slid down her back in slow motion, leaving a thick white trail of cream cheese frosting.

●

The Parents' Day Handicap was won by Mr. Fleischman, though he himself knew nothing about it. Instead of the allotted four minutes about the activities of the science department, he spoke for a record fourteen, waxing enthusiastic about his new kitchen science unit and how the eleventh grade now had a vital appreciation of the ways chemistry affected our daily lives. He was hoping his new way of connecting the sciences to the world in which we live would serve as a model for the courses taught in the other grades. He even got out a jar of mayonnaise "made by our own Katarina Dolgen during a lesson on emulsification and the stability of mixtures" and spread it on a piece of whole-grain bread he had stored in his pocket, then took three bites of it in front of everybody.

Some parents grumbled that this cooking in the classroom sounded like elementary-school work, while others complained that mayo alone on bread was disgusting, and a third group pointed out that as head of the science department, Fleischman was supposed to be lecturing not just on Chem but on Biology, Sex Ed, Physics and various electives.

Still, in terms of the Handicap, Fleischman was a clear winner, even before the head of the English department spoke, so I snuck out of the auditorium and went back to the Baby CHuBS table to set up for the final hour of the day. Meghan was still inside, sitting with her mom, and the hallway seemed eerie and empty.

There was a white sheet over the bake sale table to indicate it was temporarily closed. I pulled it off and began clearing crumbs, consolidating pastries, and setting out napkins. I got the cash box out of the locker we stored it in and began to count.

Four hundred and sixty-six dollars. In one day.

We had raised four hundred and sixty-six dollars! I had banked on three hundred, maybe three fifty.

I sat there, glowing. By the time the day was over we'd probably have five hundred dollars to give to Happy Paws. With no cuteness, a roly-poly leader and a campaign against antiquated notions of masculinity.

"We have a winner, eh?" It was Jackson, likewise cutting out of the auditorium early after Fleischman's victory. "Good for me, too, as he was no long shot."

"What were his odds?"

"Four to one, but Kline was the favorite, and way more people bet on her than on Fleischman. I think mainly juniors bet on him, 'cause you guys have had him for all the kitchen science stuff." Jackson came and sat next to me, pulling a large wad of cash from his pocket and shuffling through it under the table, putting twenties on the bottom and singles on top. "I shouldn't have to pay out too much. Kyle's gonna be mad. He bet a pile on Harada at twenty to one."

He touched my leg and a jolt went through my body.

"Hey there, you," he said, as if he'd just noticed we were alone.

"Hey."

"Can I ask you something?"

"Yeah. But you're not getting a free molten chocolate cake. Those are selling for four dollars each."

"It's not about baked goods." Jackson's thumb rubbed a small circle on my thigh.

"Oh," I said. "What's it about?"

"You." Jackson looked into my face with his beautiful

clear eyes. I knew each freckle on his nose, the square angle of his jaw, the way one bottom tooth overlapped another. "You and me."

"Isn't that ancient history?" I asked, but I didn't move my leg out from under his hand. "Or maybe Greek tragedy?"

"Does it have to be?"

He was so close. The center of my treasure map. "What are you saying?" I asked.

"I'm saying, will you go to Spring Fling with me?" He looked down shyly. "Do you want to give me another chance?"

I was so shocked I didn't speak.

This was Jackson Clarke, my first boyfriend.

This was Jackson Clarke, who looked so good without his shirt on.

This was Jackson Clarke, who had met my parents and made me laugh and picked me up every day after swim practice.

This was Jackson Clarke, who had stomped on my heart, jerked me around, run off with my best friend and then turned into a pod-robot.

This was Jackson Clarke, looking vulnerable and nervous. This was Jackson Clarke, who was such a good kisser.

This was Jackson Clarke, who wanted me back.

"I mean, I know the dance was a disaster last year," he said. "But I was hoping I could make it up to you."

I still couldn't talk.

"Maybe I can make a lot of things up to you," Jackson

continued. "Will you let me try, Roo? Because I'd really like to. I've been thinking about it since that day I ran into you with Dempsey at Nordstrom. And then I heard something about you and Noel DuBoise, probably just a rumor, but—I don't know. I couldn't stand that it wasn't me."

Here was the moment I'd been fantasizing about in my less mentally stable moments for almost a year: I could have him again. We could be in love. I could go to Spring Fling and wear a corsage and slow dance and look at the moonlight on the water.

Everything bad that had happened since Jackson dumped me could be erased, and I would finally be happy again.

Except.

Ag.

Hello?

I am insane, but I am not that insane. I had had nearly a year of therapy by now, and even though Doctor Z was the lover of an aging hippie with horrible foot fungus, I couldn't help seeing her patient brown face looking at me as those thoughts ran through my mind. She'd see the holes in my fantasy as fast as I could verbalize it.

Even as I felt the warmth of Jackson's hand on my leg, even as part of me wanted to kiss him and give him a free molten chocolate cake just for wanting me, I had to admit the following:

1. I would not "finally be happy again." I don't have a predilection for happiness. I have a predilection for anxiety. Maybe it was easy for me to be happy once, a long time ago, but something shifted in my brain. Now

it's hard. And there is no simple solution to getting happy if you're not wired for it. As Doctor Z has told me again and again: no happiness fairy is going to fly down and make everything fine; and just because the happiness fairy seems to be six feet tall and desperately cute and touches your leg, that's no reason to believe he really exists.

2. If I went to Spring Fling with Jackson, all the badness that had happened in the past year would *not* be erased. The words about me on the bathroom wall would still be there. I'd still be without my zoo job. I'd still have panic attacks and have to go to the shrink and eat almond-pumpkin pâté for dinner. Same me, same life.

3. I also wouldn't magically become friends again with Kim and Nora. Both of them would actually hate me even more than they already did, and Cricket, Katarina, Ariel and Heidi would do the same, just to keep the others company.

4. Jackson asked me to Spring Fling because he felt jealous of me kissing Noel in the art studio. He and Noel had never liked each other. They were competitive on the cross-country team. Part of this sounded like a territory battle between the two of them, not anything really about me.

5. Fact: Jackson was the guy who idealized what he didn't have. The fish that got away. The road not taken. The grass on the other side of the fence.

6. Fact: Jackson cheated on Kim when she was in Tokyo.

7. Probability: Jackson cheated on me with Kim.

8. Fact: It is a bad idea to date a known cheater, because even if he doesn't cheat on you, you will always know he's capable of it and will never fully trust him. Then you will become even more insecure and neurotic than you already are.

9. Fact: If I went to Spring Fling with Jackson, Noel would write me off forever.

If he hadn't already.

But if I wanted Jackson, I argued with myself, if he was at the center of my treasure map, shouldn't I just take him, now that I could suddenly have him?

Sure, it wouldn't solve everything.

Sure, it would cause more angst in some ways. But wouldn't I have love? For a little while, at least?

And wasn't that something?

These ideas sped through my mind in a tremendous rush, but as Jackson took his hand off my leg and reached to touch my hair, I told him, "No. I'm sorry. I can't."

Oh.

That wasn't what I thought I was going to say.

Most of me was leaning toward saying yes and going to the dance and having love.

But out it came: "No. I'm sorry. I can't."

Jackson pulled back. Surprised. "Oh. Okay."

"I just—I don't want to get involved with you, Jackson," I said, the words tumbling out. "You're a nice guy, but then, when it comes down to it—you're not, really."

"Not what?"

"Not nice."

"That's not true."

"I think it might be," I said.

"Look." Jackson leaned back in his chair. "I know I've done some stupid things in the past. I know I wasn't the best boyfriend to you—or to anyone. But I was confused. I was confused for a long time. And I think I've finally figured out what I need."

"What you need?"

"You." He set his chair legs on the floor and leaned toward me again. "That's why I've logged all this time at your bake sale table."

I shook my head. "You needed somewhere to operate the Handicap."

"Please," he laughed. "I could operate it in the refectory easier than anyplace else. I was trying to get near you again and I needed an excuse."

Oh. "But why?"

"You're not like Kim," he answered after a beat. "She's so controlling and insecure. Most girls are. But you, you don't care what people think. You have so much self-confidence. Plus, you're beautiful, and we were good together, Roo. You know we were."

Everything he said sounded wonderful, but it wasn't true. I was desperately insecure and I did care what people thought. Jackson wasn't really talking about me. He was talking about an *idea* of me he'd concocted in his head. As soon as he remembered me and my true weaknesses in the clear light of day, he'd be as cruel this time as he had been the last.

"So will you think about it?" Jackson asked, stroking my hair.

I stood and shook his hand off. "I don't need to think about it," I said—although part of me was still screaming *Think about it! Think about it!* "You turned into a pod-robot. Not even Cricket turned into a pod-robot. At least she was mean to me. At least she had feelings. You were just completely cold, as if we'd never even known each other. As if nothing had ever happened between us. I don't want to be with *anyone* who could act like that."

"I'm sorry," he said sarcastically. "Just because I don't *show* my feelings to the whole Tate Universe, all the time every day, doesn't mean I don't *have* them."

"I'm sure you have feelings, Jackson," I told him. "I just don't think they're very deep."

"Fuck you."

"See?" I said. "That's exactly the person I don't want to be with. And he's always there, underneath all your charm."

"If that's what you think," he said, "I don't need to be here." He shoved his notebook into his backpack, slung the bag over his shoulder, grabbed a molten chocolate cake without paying for it—and walked off without a word.

I did not have a panic attack.

I didn't even have trouble breathing.

I sat at the Baby CHuBS table until people came streaming out of the auditorium, and then I sold deliciousness until we had five hundred and seventeen dollars to donate to Happy Paws.

19.

I Reveal the Treasure Map

Dear Robespierre,

How have you been?

I have been completely rotten and I miss scratching you behind your ears.

We have a dog now: a Great Dane called Polka-dot. He is an idiot, but his heart is in the right place and his ears want scratching. I think the two of you would get on together well. You're both inclined to eat things you aren't supposed to eat. (Do you long for the sleeve of my green hoodie?)

Anyway: I was wondering, Robespierre, do you ever get in fights with Kaczynski over the lady goats? Like, if you want to be with Mata Hari, and so does he, do you butt your heads in fury? Or does one of you back down and let the other one win?

How do you work it out? Because I know you all have to live to-gether in the indoor pen at night when the zoo is closed. Do you and Kaczynski forget your differences? Does one of you say sorry?

Please write back as soon as you can. Which I do understand is probably never.

—Ruby Oliver

—written by me and mailed to the Woodland Park Zoo, with a note on the envelope reading: "For the 'Write to Our Farm Animals!' box."

the next day was Saturday and I felt like crying all morning. I wasn't sure why, except that things had ended.

Baby CHuBS.

The Parents' Day Handicap.

Whatever had been going on with Jackson.

I didn't have to be at Granola Brothers until two pm, so I walked Polka-dot down to this place in our neighbor-hood that has coffee drinks and got a banana muffin and a vanilla cappuccino. Polka-dot licked my muffin halfway through, so I let him have it.

I looked into his joyful, doggy face, dripping with slobber and good humor, and I had to admit I loved him, even though the way my parents dealt with him was certi-fiably neurotic. I massaged his soft ears and let him eat my paper napkin.

Animals. I missed Robespierre. And the llamas Laverne and Shirley. Imelda, Mata Hari, Kaczynski and Anne Boleyn. The pig Lizzie Borden.

I even missed the penguins, though they never paid me any attention.

It was just a sad morning.

When I got home I dragged the treasure map out of my closet and stared at it.

Jackson, there in the center with a lollipop in his mouth, grinning.

Finn, who hadn't been crushing on me after all.

Noel, who wasn't speaking to me.

Gideon, who was Nora's brother and therefore hated me now.

I had written: "Someone who doesn't care if my hair looks stupid."

"Something uncomplicated."

"Something real."

"Wanting guys you can't have is a recipe for unhappiness. Do not fall for people who hardly know you exist."

"Liking a guy just because *he* likes *you*: Is that immature and pitiful, or is that a smart interpersonal relationship strategy likely to result in true happiness?"

"Do not think about guys who have broken your heart six ways. It is mentally deranged to chase after heartbreak."

And: "Say you'll be my partner true/In Chemistry, it's me and you."

What a stupid set of contradictory statements. And what a stupid set of guys to be spending my time thinking about. The whole thing was idiotic.

None of them gave a crap about me anyway. Jackson was a cheater/pod-robot and I couldn't believe I'd been thinking about him so much when I was supposed to have gotten over him ages ago. I ripped his photograph off the treasure map and tore it in half.

Noel. He'd made out with Ariel and let me down for the bake sale and didn't listen when I tried to explain about Jackson. He'd also abandoned me during the storm of gossip after Ariel found us kissing in the art studio—so whatever he'd felt couldn't be much, now could it?

No.

Do not think about guys who have broken your heart six ways. It is mentally deranged to chase after heartbreak.

I was crying, my eyes leaking and my nose running, and was digging through my desk for my scissors so I could cut up the map, when my dad tapped on the door.

"I'll come out in a minute," I called, but he knocked again.

"Hold on!" I set the scissors on the desk and rummaged under my bed for a box of tissues. I blew my nose and wiped my eyes and put some powder on my face. If I had any luck Dad would just be asking some inane question like did I do my French homework, when it was only Saturday morning. He wouldn't notice I'd been crying.

"Okay, come in!" I told him—but it wasn't Dad. It was Hutch. He'd been helping out in the greenhouse when I got home with Polka-dot.

"Hey," he said, standing in the doorway. "Sorry to bother you." In practically a whole year working at our house, he'd never entered my room.

I sniffed. "No problem. What do you want?"

"I, um." He picked at his fingernails. "I could, uh, tell you were upset when you got home, so I wanted to see if you were okay."

"I'm not upset," I said. "How could you tell I was upset?"

Hutch shrugged. "Usually you come say hi to us in the greenhouse, or at least you yell a derogatory comment about plant life."

I smiled. That was true.

But who knew Hutch even noticed anything I usually did?

"This time," he went on, "you moped into the house like you had something weighing on you, and I heard your door slam. Your dad called for you to come out and look at the new planters we bought at the nursery, but you didn't even seem to hear him."

"Oh." It was strange having Hutch in my room. He wasn't wearing the Iron Maiden leather jacket he wore to school no matter what the weather—just a gray Skid Row T-shirt and jeans with planting soil on them. "You can sit if you want." I gestured at the chair by my desk.

"When you didn't come back out," Hutch said, sitting down, "after a while I thought I'd knock."

"That was nice of you, but I'm okay," I told him. "I'm just having, you know, a sucky life right now."

Hutch looked at the treasure map next to him. "What's this?" he asked.

I wanted to lie and say it was an art project for school, but he was looking at it carefully. I stared at him, sitting at my desk with his pimply, pockmarked skin and greasy hair and his general awkward Hutch-ness, and I couldn't make the lie come out. "It's a treasure map of boys," I said. "You're not allowed to laugh."

His eyes crinkled. "Okay."

"I mean it, no laughing."

"No laughing," he said. "But admit: it does sound a *little bit* funny."

"It sounds *insane* is what it sounds," I told him, "but it's this thing my shrink made me do. You know I see a shrink, right?"

"Your dad might have mentioned it." This was Hutch being polite, as Dad was all too inclined to say things like "John, Ruby's therapist is working with her on anxiety management, but she still covers her emotions with obnoxious statements about the dullness of container gardening, so you can take what she says with a few grains of salt, 'kay?" If you hung around with my folks for more than half an hour, you were sure to know their kid was in therapy. They believed in being open about these things even with people they barely knew.

"Yeah," I said. "So the shrink gave me this treasure map assignment and I'm supposed to be sorting out all my crap personal relationships and visualizing how they might be better, only I did it all wrong."

"Wrong, how?"

"It was supposed to be about my peer group and friends and stuff, and instead I did it just about boys, because I'm obsessed or something, possibly certifiable. Again, don't laugh."

Hutch didn't laugh.

215

I babbled on: "Then everything went wrong with my shrink because she has this boyfriend with gross feet and I met him and now I can't even talk to her about anything anymore. So I never showed the map to her or redid it the right way. Now I realize none of it makes any sense and none of the people on it would ever want me anyway—or the only one who *does* is an egotistical pod-robot and just wants me because he doesn't have me."

Hutch nodded. But he looked confused.

"I sound like a madman, don't I?" I wished I'd kept my mouth shut.

"I'm a boy," Hutch finally said, looking at the treasure map. "But I'm not on here."

"God," I said, sniffling. "Why would you even *want* to be on there?"

He stood up and shoved his hands in his pockets. "Obviously there's nothing romantic between you and me, but we are French partners, Ruby. We do eat lunch sometimes, and we do hang out in the greenhouse like a couple times a week."

"Yeah?"

"So. I feel dumb saying this, but I don't have a very long list of friends, and you're on it. That short list that I have. So I thought I might be on your map."

Oh.

That was true.

And it must have been really hard to say.

I had spent weeks feeling like I had only one friend in the Tate Universe and that was Meghan. But here was another one, standing right in my house. Right in my bedroom.

He just didn't look how I thought my friends looked. How my friends used to look.

This was what Doctor Z meant about a treasure map. I was supposed to find the treasure in my own life, and map out how I might dig deeper and get more of it.

Hutch had brought me a surprise cappuccino that time.

And now I had hurt his feelings.

"I'm sorry," I said. "Sometimes I'm not a very good friend."

He shrugged.

I took a Sharpie and sketched in a small free space on the map. "That's you, see, with the Skid Row T-shirt— here's your arm, here's your other arm. You're holding a plant. Okay, not a very good-looking plant, but a plant."

Hutch laughed.

"Now here are legs, and feet, and I'm drawing a box around you to make it clear you're not part of all the insanity going on with all the rest of these guys. Good?"

"I look bald," said Hutch.

"Okay, I'll give you a little more hair." I scribbled it in. "Do you like it?"

"Now my hair is enormous."

"You see? Being on my treasure map is not all you imagined it would be," I said. "In fact, it kind of sucks. But now you're on it and there's no taking you off."

"I guess I asked for it," he said, smiling.

"Do you want to go to Spring Fling with me?" I

blurted. "You know, as friends. We could dress up and eat somewhere fancy. It'd be fun. And even though we wouldn't have *date* dates, we wouldn't miss the dance?"

Hutch coughed. "I. Ah . . ."

"What?"

"Honestly, I *want* to miss the dance."

"You do?"

"Those things always make me feel like a loser."

Oh.

"Like my clothes aren't right and I can't dance."

"You wear a suit, the clothes won't be a problem," I said.

Hutch shook his head. "What I mean is, I don't like most of the people at Tate, anyway, so fuck it. Why go somewhere that makes you feel bad if you don't have to go there to get your education? The last dance I even *tried* going to was in seventh grade."

Oh.

He was being truthful with me.

"All right, let's not go, then," I told him. "It sounds like you'd really hate it."

"I do have an extra ticket to see Van Halen at KeyArena that night," Hutch said. "Noel was going to go with me, but then he realized Spring Fling was the same time. So, ah. We could do that if you want. My parents bought the tickets. It wouldn't cost you anything."

"Yeah," I said. "That would be excellent. I could use a little retro-metal therapy."

"A little what?"

"Never mind. Do you think David Lee Roth will wear spandex and take his shirt off?"

"He might," said Hutch. "But now *you* have to promise not to laugh."

"Okay," I said. "But admit: David Lee Roth is a *little bit* funny."

"I admit nothing," said Hutch. "He's a rock legend."

We got Popsicles out of the back of the freezer and ate them in the greenhouse with my dad, listening to Van Halen sing "Jump." And I thought: This is my treasure. My ridiculous dad and my oddball friend Hutch, rocking out with purple mouths from the grape Popsicles, in this room full of flowering plants.

Not everybody has this.

●

Polka-dot misbehaved in the Honda on the way to the Woodland Park Zoo. He liked to stick his giant head out the window and bark like a lunatic at all the other cars. I wonder if he thought they were other Great Danes. They weren't that much bigger than him.

Dogs aren't allowed inside the zoo, but I was only going to be a few minutes, so I tied him outside the entrance. No one would ever try to steal Polka-dot. He's too enormous to even chance it. I mean, he is a superfriendly guy, but he looks as if he could bite your head off. And he might—if he thought there was a good chance you'd taste like a homemade doughnut.

I found Anya, my old boss, sitting in her office shuffling papers and wearing a pinched expression. "Ruby," she said crisply when I poked my head in the door. "How can I help you?"

"May I come in?"

"Certainly."

It was impossible to make small talk with Anya—she was an all-business person—so I told her why I'd come: "I want my job back."

"We don't just give jobs back because people ask," Anya said. "You lost your internship for a good reason."

"I know."

"There are other people working your stations now," she said.

"I realize that."

"Then I'm not sure what you expect me to do, Ruby." Anya tapped her pen on the desk as if to show me I was wasting her time.

I didn't think she wanted to hear anything I had to say, but I was going to say it anyway.

"I miss the job a huge amount," I explained. "I miss the animals. I miss their smells. I miss feeling connected to something outside the universe of my school. I miss being cranked to go to work and caring whether I've done well."

"That's all very nice, but you were negligent in surveying the area for which you were responsible, and you were unforgivably rude to one of our patrons," Anya replied.

"If you want to take me out of Family Farm customer interaction, that's fine," I said. "I don't have to do the penguin talk anymore either. You can put me back on planting duty and mucking out farm stalls so I don't have any contact with people who come to the zoo. Or you can have me go through training again."

Anya's pen stopped tapping.

"Any way you want to work it," I continued. "But I'm really hoping you'll give me another chance."

She looked at me with her tiny brown eyes and ran her tongue over her braces.

"Please?" I said.

"Lewis does need assistance with the spring plantings," she said finally.

"Great."

"And I have another intern who wants to move out of mucking the farm stalls into an activity that's more patron-oriented."

"I'll do it," I said. "I don't mind."

"We want someone to work Sundays, too," she told me. "None of my interns wants to work Sundays."

"Sundays are fine."

"You'd be on probation for a month," said Anya.

"You mean I have the job?"

She didn't smile, but she held out her hand for me to shake. "Wednesdays four to seven, Saturdays twelve to five and Sundays nine to one. You start next week."

When I left the office, I went straight to the Family Farm to see Robespierre and the llamas. Laverne and Shirley snubbed me, acting as if they'd never seen me before in their lives and looking at me snootily through lidded eyes, but Robespierre remembered me. He rubbed his ears up against my hand and snarfled my palm. I bought him a handful of farm food and he ate it greedily. Then I wrote him another letter on park stationery.

Dear Robespierre,
    I'm back! Did you miss me? I'll be mucking out your pen Wednesday nights and Sunday mornings, and scratching your head on a regular basis.
    I promise to wear the hoodie you like.
    Ruby Oliver

When Polka-dot saw me coming through the front gates, he stood on his hind legs and barked with joy, wagging his tail and slobbering and terrifying a group of small children, one of whom cried, "Mean pony, mean pony!" and burst into tears.

I stroked Polka-dot's neck and told him what a handsome guy he was. Then the two of us squeezed into the Honda and drove away.

●

Tuesday I brought my treasure map to Doctor Z's office. She raised her eyebrows when I walked in with the big sheet of watercolor paper, but she didn't say anything except "Hello, Ruby. Have a seat."

"I'm really freaked out that I met your boyfriend," I blurted.

"Oh?" She reached for the Nicorette and popped a piece of gum out of the packaging.

"Jonah was nice," I said—because he was—"but it was way too much information. Now I'm all spazzed out in therapy and I haven't been able to tell you anything that's been going on, like how I kissed Noel and everyone hates me again, and I'm shattered about Nora and Noel maybe going out together, and Jackson asked me to Spring Fling and I said no, and–I haven't said anything about any of it, because whenever I want to start talking, I keep thinking about how you have this whole life outside the office and then nothing comes out of my mouth."

"It's true," said Doctor Z. "I do have a life outside the office."

"I know. Ag."

"Usually my clients don't come across me in my other life, but now and then, we run into one another. Feeling unsettled by an encounter like that is a natural part of the therapeutic situation."

"Were you spazzed out too, then?"

She looked at me but didn't answer.

"Were you?"

"Yes," she admitted. "On principle I don't reveal my private relationships to clients. But Jonah is–he's gregarious. And he'd been talking to you quite a while before I got there."

"Yeah, he's chatty," I said.

"He likes the sandals very much."

I bit my fingernail. "I didn't think you were going to answer me about being spazzed out, actually."

"Why not?"

"You don't admit to emotions. You just get *me* to admit to emotions. That's your job, isn't it?"

Doctor Z laughed. "I'm not a pod-robot, Ruby."

"Ha!" I said. "You got that word from me. That's not a shrink term, *pod-robot*. That's a Ruby Oliver term."

"I listen to you carefully," said Doctor Z. "It's my job to be paying attention."

And that was true. She did listen carefully.

"I feel like this whole thing we do each week, I feel like it's one-sided," I said. "You know nearly everything about me and I know nothing about you. Isn't that sick and unbalanced?"

"It's therapy," said Doctor Z. "It's a methodology."

"I wanted to know all these things about you. I had so many questions. And then when I actually knew something—I really, really didn't want to know," I told her.

"That's probably healthy."

"You mean I have actual evidence of mental health?"

"Sure. We've been over this before, Ruby. You're far from crazy."

"But I am having all these panic attacks," I said. "I keep having them. And I have no one to talk to, because my parents are supremely annoying and Meghan has a new boyfriend. So everything is smashed up inside me and it's making me *feel* crazy." I sniffed. "The attacks are really scary. And the retro-metal cure isn't working."

"So let's work on that," Doctor Z replied. "I'm here to help."

I showed her my half-finished, half-destroyed treasure map, and told her everything that had happened. *Everything*.

She took the map and looked at it closely. "I know I did it wrong," I told her.

"Actually," she replied, "I don't think you did it wrong at all. This is a sincere and complicated expression of what you've been thinking and going through."

Yeah. That was true.

"But wasn't I supposed to have girls on it?" I said. "I should be valuing my peer group and relationships beyond the romantic, right? I shouldn't be so obsessed with boys."

Doctor Z chuckled. "We don't need to put that label 'shouldn't' on it," she told me. "You are sixteen years old and heterosexual, after all."

"So?"

"So a little obsession with boys is natural."

Then I told her what I'd realized about the treasure in the grape Popsicles with Hutch and Dad in the greenhouse, and she said, "We're seeing some alteration in the way you're framing things, don't you think?"

And I thought, Yeah, maybe we are.

And maybe I figured something out on my own.

And maybe I'm not such a bad friend after all.

But what I said was: "That has got to be the shrinkiest thing you've ever said to me in a whole year of head shrinking."

Doctor Z laughed.

When our time was up, I didn't feel better, exactly.

But I felt lighter.

20.

I Want to Be Treated Like a Dog,
Strange As That Sounds

They came out kinda flat, and
They came out kinda greasy.
I made them really, really late,
And honestly—they're not that great.

But:
They took me several hours,
There's a burn across my thumb,
Then I had to clean the kitchen,
Now I want to give you some.

—written on an index card taped to a shoe box delivered to my doorstep, early June of junior year.

Spring Fling came and went without me. I was at Van Halen with Hutch. David Lee Roth took his shirt off and wore spandex. It was gross and thrilling at the same time. Hutch banged his head around and jumped up and down like a heavy-metal lunatic. It would have been embarrassing to be next to him, except everyone in KeyArena was doing the same thing, so finally I went with it and banged my head around too, even though there were lots of songs I didn't know.

Driving home, all of Seattle seemed quiet. It was late at night, and there was a slight drizzle. The streets were shining. The world seemed cinematic.

Hutch and I got pizza and argued about the guitar skills of Eddie Van Halen versus Kirk Hammett, then Angus Young versus Slash.[1] I had no idea what I was talking about, but it was fun to take the opposite position to Hutch and watch him get worked up. He defended Slash to the end.

Meghan called me around noon the next day and told me all about Spring Fling. She and Finn had kissed under the stars as the mini-yacht cruised across the lake. She thought she might be in love. Before the dance, they had dinner at Waterfront Seafood Grill with Noel and Nora, two soccer muffins and their dates: Varsha and Spencer. Nora looked beautiful. Noel wore a vintage suit. Meghan ate salmon with cilantro sauce and chocolate cake. The boys tried to order wine but the waiter wouldn't serve them.

---

[1] Do you really want to know the difference between these guitarists? Nah.

I felt a surge of jealousy, thinking about Nora and Noel going to the dance. Yes, Meghan said, in answer to my question, they talked and laughed and seemed to be having a good time.

A really good time? I asked.

Yes. Noel was being so funny at dinner.

Did they hold hands or anything?

They danced. She's taller than him, but she wore flats, so it wasn't too bad.

Did it get romantic? I wanted to know.

"I can't get in the middle here between you and Nora," Meghan said. "But she didn't call in the morning and say she'd kissed him. I still don't think he likes her back the same way, but it was hard to tell at Spring Fling, you know? With the starlight and the music and everyone looking so gorgeous."

Did—

But Meghan didn't want to talk about Nora and Noel. She wanted to talk about her and Finn. Most people went to an after-party at the Yamamotos' after the dance, but Meghan had driven Finn home instead and there had been some serious upper-regioning. She wondered if Finn was inexperienced, though. She herself was well acquainted with the nether regions, but Finn seemed shy, she said, and wasn't that sweet?

I tried to listen and even ask questions that had nothing to do with Noel and Nora, because I was happy for Meghan, I really was, and I wanted to be a good friend. But my mind was running.

If my life was a movie, I figured, Noel would be the

hero. I used to think it would be Jackson, because there I had a classic plot: Girl meets boy, they fall in love; girl loses boy, misery; girl gets boy back again, happy ending. But even though Jackson had once been exactly what I wanted—even though we had once been happy—I knew now that I didn't want him anymore.

Noel was the one whose kisses were better than retro metal. He was the one who made me laugh all through Chem class and wrote me that note I copied onto my treasure map. He was the one who had misunderstood something and thought I didn't care about him (girl loses boy)—and he was the one who seemed to have gone off with someone else (misery). So if my life was a movie, it was now time for "girl gets boy back again" and "happy ending"—which meant one of these three things would happen:

1. Nora would turn out to be evil. I would uncover some sinister plot she was hatching and foil it using emulsions. Noel would realize Nora was evil, admire me for my heroic deeds and show up at my house saying: "I came here tonight because when you realize you want to spend the rest of your life with somebody, you want the rest of your life to start as soon as possible."[2] Then the two of us would stroll into the sunset, and for once, his hair would look cool.

2. Nora would fall wildly in love with a basketball muffin who appreciated her sporty nature and her photography skills. She would see that she was wrong

---

[2] What Billy Crystal says to Meg Ryan in *When Harry Met Sally*.

to be mad at me for kissing Noel and beg my forgiveness. She would tell Noel he was wrong to be mad at me for hugging Jackson, and Noel would show up at my house saying: "I am just a boy standing in front of a girl, asking her to love him."[3] He'd also beg my forgiveness by sending me flowers and serenading me outside my window, singing a medley of songs by Joe Cocker and Elton John.[4] Then he and I would stroll into the sunset wearing excellent vintage outfits.

3. Nora would realize she is a lesbian and confess she had been hiding her true nature from herself by imagining her crush on Noel when really he was just a nearby male for whom she had no true romantic feelings. Jackson would turn out to be evil, revealing that he'd been telling Noel lies about me—which would mean that Noel didn't think I was a complete slut after all. Noel would realize he'd wronged me terribly, and he'd show up at my house saying, "You complete me."[5] Then we'd drive into the sunset on Noel's Vespa, our hair blowing in the wind because in movies you never have to wear an ugly helmet.

Of course, life doesn't happen like that. In life, even if someone says "You complete me," his hair still looks funny. Or he has a bad cold. Or even though you com-

---

[3] What Julia Roberts says to Hugh Grant in *Notting Hill*—only with the sexes reversed.
[4] The way Ewan McGregor does for Nicole Kidman in *Moulin Rouge*.
[5] What Tom Cruise says to Renée Zellweger in *Jerry Maguire*.

plete him, he still blows you off the next day to watch a basketball game with the guys.

And in life, you *do* have to choose between your friend and the boy you like. She doesn't magically fall in love with someone else, realize she's gay or turn out evil. No one turns out to be evil. People are complicated and make mistakes. They're thoughtless, selfish womanizers who can turn into pod-robots at a moment's notice—but they're also funny and kind sometimes when you've been crying (Jackson). Or they're stubborn and self-righteous and un-forgiving, but also generous and honest and they take care of you when you're having a panic attack (Nora).

They're not ideal and romantic, either. They're hand-some and good kissers and above all *interesting,* but they're insensitive about things like asking you to be a bodyguard, and they don't believe you when you try to explain why you were hugging someone else (Noel).

231

Or they're hyperverbal and reasonably good-looking, and they mean well and they're good with animals, and they can put on a damn good bake sale, but they get con-fused about what and whom they want, and all too often can't resist temptation (me).

In life, maybe you do eventually find love, but it's not with your high school boyfriend. It's with a completely different person whom you never even met before—some-one who didn't figure into the first part of the story at all. In life, there's no happily-ever-after-into-the-sunset. There's a marriage, complete with arguments, bad hair, lost hair, mentally unstable children, weird diets, dogs that fur up the couch, not enough money. Like my parents. That's their life I just described—but then, there they were, talking on the phone about my dad massaging my mom's groin area after yoga; cuddling on the couch; holding hands and wearing stupid Great Dane paraphernalia.

That's all we can realistically hope for. In fact, I think it's as close to happily-ever-after as things get. Though I am not yet sure if I find that fact depressing or encouraging.

The next Tuesday, when I told Doctor Z all these thoughts I'd been having, she asked me if I wanted to be friends with Nora.

I hadn't put it to myself that way, as a question.

Did I?

Did I?

I was mad that she was only friends with me so long as I kept my hands off Noel. Even though it took like four months for her to ask him out. Even though, aside from agreeing to go to Spring Fling, he'd never given her any evidence of liking her back, and in fact had been

1. writing me sexy notes about Chemistry

2. giving me candy rings and

3. full-out kissing me.

I loved Nora. I had loved her for a long time, and there was still so much to love about her. But she didn't really love me back, did she? She had dropped me twice (once now, once sophomore year) rather than trying to understand why I'd acted the way I did. She had been furious about me and Noel without even listening to my side of it—because even though we were friends, she still basically thought of me as a boyfriend stealer.

She didn't allow me any room to behave any way but the way she wanted me to.

My family didn't get rid of Polka-dot when he ate our doughnuts. We didn't get rid of him when his tail knocked Great-grandpa's antique clock off the credenza. We didn't get rid of him because he furred up the couch or had indigestion or slobbered on our baked goods so we couldn't eat them. No, we took him on car rides even when he misbehaved and we bought stupid shirts and tote bags saying how much we loved him.

Of course we scolded him. We said "No, Polka-dot!" and tied him on the dock if he was farting. Maybe we even slapped his nose once in a while. But we told him we were mad and then we forgave him. Because our attitude was generally: Polka-dot is good. Polka-dot is loved. If Polka-dot is a huge pain to live with once in a while, we'll deal with it, because the good outweighs the bad.

I wanted a friend who felt about me the way my family felt about Polka-dot. That's what I told Doctor Z. I used to think Kim was that friend, but now there was no way we'd ever be anything to each other again.

Were we ever true friends, then, since it had ended so badly?

Yes, actually. We were. Before boys and Mocha Latte came between us. Before we both wanted the same thing. Before, before.

Now Meghan might be that kind of solid friend. Sometimes I didn't understand her, and a lot of times she didn't understand me, but she cut me slack. And I cut her some.

Nora wasn't a true friend in that way. Or she hadn't been in a long time, and I didn't know if she'd ever come back around to loving me like I loved Polka-dot. Maybe she would if I just gave it time. If circumstances changed again.

Maybe.

●

May was uneventful. It rained and Seattle turned emerald green. I watched the girls' lacrosse team play a few times. I took the SATs.

During carpool and on weekday afternoons when Finn worked or played soccer, I hung out with Meghan, but most of the time at school she had become half of Finn&Meghan, just as sophomore year she'd been half of Meghan&Bick. She kissed Finn in the refectory, sat on his lap and made a spectacle of herself.

She ate with the boy soccer muffins at lunch most days, leaving me to either join them (awkward) or sit alone (more awkward), since Hutch was usually with Noel. On weekends she had taken over my job at Granola Brothers, since now I worked at the zoo, and at night she was always with Finn and sometimes with Nora—so really, I hardly saw her.

It's not that she was ditching me. It's that Meghan was the kind of girl whose world centered around her boyfriend. She always had been, and she probably always would be. She was the girl who ate lunch all sophomore year at a table full of seniors who didn't like her, oblivious because Bick's shining smile was the only thing she could see. So I wasn't surprised, or even mad, that she became half of Finn&Meghan. That was who she was.

I was grateful, though, for my schedule at the zoo. It kept me from noticing how alone I usually was on weekends.

One day in late May, when Hutch was working for my dad, he brought over this documentary, *Dream Deceivers*. It's about how these two teenagers shot themselves after a Judas Priest concert–Judas Priest being a retro-metal band that was one of Hutch's favorites. The boys' families and the legal team they hired tried to put the blame on the band, claiming subliminal messages in their lyrics had mesmerized the kids into a suicide pact.

These people obviously had no understanding of the secret mental health of hair bands. Anyway, the movie was superinteresting, and after watching it we decided to have a documentary film festival in my living room, to be curated by yours truly.[6]

Hutch's parents are never home, so my dad began asking him to stay for dinner. At first, when Hutch tasted my mom's zucchini-cashew loaf, I was pretty sure he was never going to eat dinner with us again–I could see the sick look on his face. So I said something I'd been meaning to say for a long time: "Mom, if we have to eat raw, couldn't we just have salad and fruit a couple nights a week? Just salad and fruit–no recipes you've found on

---

[6] We watched *March of the Penguins, Super Size Me, Spellbound, American Movie, Mad Hot Ballroom, Grizzly Man, Hoop Dreams, Shut Up & Sing*—and for Hutch, *Metallica: Some Kind of Monster.* Which is about a retro-metal band in group therapy, if you can believe it.

the Internet? No soaked raw peanuts, no banana-avocado pudding?"

Surprisingly, she said okay. Salad was acceptable, so long as the dressing was entirely raw. So Hutch stayed for dinner now and then, and after eating salad we'd watch documentaries and do our French homework at the same time.

One day I went for ice cream during a free period with Varsha from swim team. I was surprised she invited me. She's a sporty girl, plays soccer in the spring, while until this year I always did lacrosse. I've never been in her circle even though we did November Week together. She and Spencer were getting into Varsha's BMW. I was heading through the parking lot to get my sweater out of Meghan's Jeep and they waved me over.

"Ruby!" Varsha said when I stuck my head in her window. "Do you like ice cream?"

"Do pigs fly?"

It was a joke, but they didn't get it. "They have sorbet if you don't eat dairy," Spencer said.

"We're going to Mix in the U District," Varsha explained. "You in?"

"Sure," I said, opening the rear door and folding myself into the seat. I was trying to hide my surprise, so I added: "With Baby CHuBS over, now I'm having trouble keeping my sugar intake up, so I appreciate the help."

I got espresso ice cream with graham crackers mixed in. Varsha got cheesecake with strawberries, and Spencer chocolate with smashed peanut-butter cups. We had to eat in the car on the way back to school so we wouldn't miss class, but it was some serious deliciousness anyway.

As the lowest-status person, I was in the backseat as Varsha sped down the highway licking her ice cream cone and blasting what I think was Hillary Duff. I stared out the back window of the car at Mount Rainier looming above the city and wondered: If I wasn't going to try to reconcile with Nora or Noel, why didn't I make new friends? True, a ridiculous number of people at Tate Prep were Future Doctors of America who didn't much interest me, but had I put any effort into hanging out with them?

Take Varsha. She'd stood up for me once earlier in the year. She'd delivered her baked goods to Baby CHuBS. She swam a wicked butterfly and had no shame about singing Hillary Duff lyrics at the top of her lungs. Maybe she wasn't the wittiest, most ironic person. Maybe she didn't always laugh at my jokes. She wanted to be a pediatrician and thought vintage clothes were dirty. Still, she was smart and nice, she didn't seem to view me as a roly-poly slut, and if I didn't like having my school social life limited to Finn&Meghan, couldn't I do something about it?

"You guys!" I yelled, over the sound of the CD.

"Yah?"

"You want to go to the B&O tomorrow after school?"

"What's the B&O?" asked Varsha.

It seemed incredible to me that she'd never been to the B&O. I'd been there every week for years. "I'll say one thing to you," I shouted. "Free white chocolate cake. At least on the days Finn Murphy works there."

"I'm in," said Varsha.

"Double in," said Spencer.

So we went. Finn was there behind the counter and he gave us free day-old cake. (Meghan was at her shrink.) Sitting with Varsha and Spencer was a little awkward, and it made me remember how fun it had been sitting with Kim and Cricket and Nora in the B&O so many days freshman and sophomore year—but we sugared ourselves up and did our homework and talked about swim-team stuff and the hotness of Mr. Wallace.

It wasn't great.

But I was glad I'd asked them.

●

One Saturday morning in early June, I stepped outside with Polka-dot and there was a shoe box on our deck. A Converse shoe box. Taped to the top was an index card with my name on it. I pulled the card off and flipped it over. There was the note:

> *They came out kinda flat, and*
> *They came out kinda greasy.*
> *I made them really, really late,*
> *And honestly—they're not that great.*
>
> *But:*
> *They took me several hours,*
> *There's a burn across my thumb,*
> *Then I had to clean the kitchen,*
> *Now I want to give you some.*

The handwriting was Noel's.

Polka-dot was going crazy with the box, nosing it and pawing it, and finally trying to eat it, cardboard and all. I took it away from him and peeked inside. Eight kinda flat, kinda greasy, pains au chocolat.

Like he had promised to make for the bake sale but never did.

Shoved inside and stained with butter was a sheet of yellow legal paper folded in quarters. I took it out and gave Polka-dot a pastry to stop his whining. Then I tucked the box inside the front door and walked the path along the lake with the dog while I read.

Roo:

You said to me once that you were not always a good friend. I am not always a good friend either.

I couldn't really deal with Ariel Olivieri and how I made out with her when I didn't want to. So that meant I couldn't deal with you.

I couldn't really deal with the questions people were asking me about what happened in the art studio, bringing up that stupid boyfriend list from sophomore year. And that meant I couldn't deal with you.

I have never been able to deal with Jackson Clarke and how he's always been taller and better-looking and cooler than me. So that meant I couldn't deal with you.

And I couldn't really deal with Nora and how she wanted me to be her boyfriend when I wasn't interested. And that meant I couldn't deal with you.

So I acted like everything was your fault. And I didn't deal with you.

Only the thing is: I want to deal with you. I meant what I said in the art studio.

I still mean it. I told Nora how I feel, too, which was hellishly awkward.

Anyway, I don't expect you to understand, since it took me so long to tell you. Way longer than it should have.

But I hope you will understand anyway.

Here are the pastries I promised.

Noel

I walked along the lake, holding the note in my hand and crying. Crying because someone had come to me rather than me going to him.

Crying because the someone was Noel. Crying because I didn't have Rabbit Fever anymore, I just wanted Noel and nobody else.

Crying because even with Hutch and Varsha and Spencer and Finn&Meghan, even with Robespierre and Polka-dot, even with Doctor Z, even with reminding myself that I did have treasure, and the treasure was all around me—I had felt alone for a long time.

Crying, even, because I knew Noel and I wouldn't ride off into the sunset. I could pretend this was a happy ending—but it wasn't the end and things wouldn't be easy. Noel and I would misunderstand each other. People would talk about us. And Nora might not ever stop being angry. Life isn't like the movies, and it can never be real and uncomplicated at the same time.

Polka-dot, who was off his leash, came running back to me and looked into my wet face with his huge eyes. He licked my hand, then trotted away for a moment and returned with a slimy stick. I threw it for him for half an hour, just absorbing the fact that Noel had made me pastries and written that note.

Absorbing the fact that sometimes, people *do* cut you slack and forgive you and want you anyway. Sometimes they do.

And when they do, even if it's not a happy ending—it is delicious.

acknowledgments

I am greatly in debt to my editor, Beverly Horowitz, and my agent, Elizabeth Kaplan, as well as the people around them who support my books so wonderfully, including Adrienne Waintraub, Tracy Lerner, Chip Gibson, Lisa Nadel, Lisa McClatchy, Rebecca Gudelis, Melissa Sarver and Kathleen Dunn.

At a crucial moment early in the writing of this book, John Green said: "Couldn't she just want a *boy*?"—and that was very helpful. Jamin Melissa Clark helped me get my Seattle details right, though I invented stuff about the Woodland Park Zoo and the B&O Espresso to suit my narrative purposes. My mom suggested the treasure map and ideas for Doctor Z's therapeutic practices.

Ayun Halliday kept me on track in the Starbucks dungeon. Bob kept me writing at top speed and rubbed ointment on all my bruises. Libba Bray was on the mommy schedule with me. Maureen Johnson talked to me about my plot when all was dark.

Sarah Mlynowski read an early draft and said "Boring!" in all the boring bits—thereby making the book immeasurably better. Lauren Myracle read a later draft and gave me lots of smiley faces and tough love.

I got my marshmallow sculpture ideas from a number of cookbooks and Web sites, including all kinds of materials by Martha Stewart and a book called *Betty Crocker Decorating Cakes and Cupcakes*. Rawfoods .com was very helpful for Elaine Oliver's recipes, and I had help with

Roo's movie lists from Cecil Castelluci, Debbie Garfinkle, Lauren Barnholdt, Sarah Mlynowski, Siobhan Vivian, Daniel Waters, Farrin Jacobs and a number of readers unknown to me who posted ideas to my blog.

My love and gratitude to my family for their support and patience.

Turn the page for a sneak peek
at what happens next . . .

real live
boyfriends*

*Yes. Boyfriends, plural.
If my life weren't complicated,
I wouldn't be Ruby Oliver.

e.lockhart
author of we were liars

Available in paperback and ebook

1.

Real Live Boyfriends!

a definition:

A real live boyfriend does not contribute to your angst.

You do not wonder if he will call.

You do not wonder whether he will kiss you.

And he does not look at his phone while you are talking, to see if anyone has texted him.

Of course he calls. He's your boyfriend!

Of course there will be kissing. He's your boyfriend!

And of course he listens. He's your real live boyfriend!

You can sit down next to him at lunch whenever you want. There's no need for mental gyrations such as: Will he want me there when he's hanging with his friends? Or will he half ignore me in order to seem golden in front of them?

Of course you can sit with him. He's your boyfriend!

You can assume you'll see him on the weekend. You can call him just to chat. You can expect he'll be nice to your friends.

Contrary to some rumors, however, you don't have to be in love. You don't have to engage in any horizontal action beyond what you're in the mood for. You don't even need to stay together after high school. But you have to like him and he has to like you—and everyone has to know you're together.

He's your real live boyfriend!

2

The Insanity of My Parents! And Romance!

from seventh grade to ninth, I had a real live boyfriend named Tommy Hazard.

Tommy was perfect. He had clear skin, he was never obnoxious in class, and he was excellent at sports. He had beautiful strong shoulders and a secret mysterious smile. Tall but not too tall. Great teeth. Smoldering eyes.

In fact, he was superhot and could have any girl he wanted. And the best thing was–he went weak whenever he saw me.

He was also imaginary.

I told my best friend, Kim, all about him. He changed according to my mood. Sometimes he was a surfer boy in board shorts and a bead choker, tossing the water out of his hair as he smiled down at me. Sometimes he was a skate punk. Other times a mod guy in a narrow tie who took beautiful black-and-white photographs.

Then I started going out with Jackson Clarke, sophomore year, and Tommy Hazard disappeared–I guess because I finally had a real live boyfriend with a real live heart pumping in his chest.

Only–then it turned out he didn't.

Have a heart.

And he didn't want to be my real live boyfriend anymore–

He wanted to be Kim's.